An Irish
Immigrant Story

Jack Cashman

PAGE PUBLISHING, INC.
New York, NY

First originally published by Page Publishing, Inc. 2018

ISBN 978-1-64350-679-1 (Paperback)
ISBN 978-1-64350-680-7 (Digital)

Printed in the United States of America

AUTHOR'S NOTE

Even for a book that is "historical fiction", a certain amount of research is required to fit historical data into the fictitious story line. The historical data in this book concerning the career of John L. Sullivan, the Irish Famine and the Irish revolution comes predominantly from the internet. Perhaps the most comprehensive book written on the "great hunger" is "Paddy's Lament", which I would recommend to anyone looking for more detail about the Famine. The referenced resources for that book as well as the book itself were also used as a resource for this book to give the reader a sense of the devastation of the Famine. It was an event that helped shape the Irish desire for independence finally resulting in the Easter Uprising and subsequent revolution. It also shaped the lives of those who came to the United States to escape the hunger. The family members they left behind faced starvation and often the immigrants who escaped never knew what became of those left behind.

Finally much of the story is also based on my own family history of which I'm very proud.

FOREWORD

America has a long and unfortunate history of poor treatment of ethnic groups who have immigrated to our great nation. The Irish immigrants of the 19th century were among those to experience this type of treatment. Help wanted signs which read, "No Irish need apply" became a lasting symbol of this treatment, as did more cruel signs like "no dogs no pigs and no Irish". One newspaper even opined that the nation could eliminate crime altogether by sending the Irish back where they came from.

In spite of it all the Irish have gained great success in America and have contributed to the success of our nation. This book is a story of one Irish family's experience and their success in overcoming the early discrimination they faced. It gives insight into the "great hunger" that drove Irish immigrants out of their country to America. It also chronicles Ireland's successful drive for independence.

This historical novel provides insight into events in both Ireland and America; it also is an enjoyable reading experience.

George J. Mitchell
Former U.S. Senate Majority Leader

PROLOGUE

Kilkenny, Ireland, February 2, 1916

A group of fourteen members of the Irish Volunteer Force surrounded the barracks of the Royal Irish Constabulary at 4:30 a.m. on a morning in February 1916. The group led by Eamon MacElaney were following orders that came from the military council leader, Thomas Clarke.

Short on arms and ammunitions, the order was given for IVF forces to raid RIC barracks to seize armaments and then destroy the barracks. This was one of three surprise raids to take place on this day, on three different barracks known to be storage centers for armaments.

The IVF force in Kilkenny included a forty-year-old Boston, Massachusetts, native named Conor Cashman. He had come to Ireland to join in the fight for independence. In Boston, he served as the head of that city's chapter of the Fenian Brotherhood, an organization that for decades had provided support for the cause of independence. On this day he would see his first front line action.

MacElaney did not have enough ammunition to engage in a down and out gun battle with the occupying constables. They would simply hold out until the IVF forces ran out of ammunition. Tensions were high so the barracks were manned twenty-four hours a day. His best information was that there were eight constables inside the barracks. He had them outmanned, plus he had the element of surprise. The plan of attack was to throw an incendiary device through the back window while at the same time busting through the front door with a battering ram carried by four of the volunteers. A second group of six would closely follow the four, ramming through the door and subduing the surprised constables.

Cashman volunteered to be one of the four members to ram through the door and be the frontline attackers. At exactly 4:30 a.m., under cover of darkness, the assault began. The incendiary device went through the window while the front door was busted open. The four men carrying the ram dropped it in favor of taking their rifles off their shoulders to prepare for action. They spread out in two directions to make room for the trailing six.

The constable on night duty responded more quickly than was anticipated. His first shot struck Sean Kelly square in the chest. He was dead before he hit the floor. A second constable burst through the door leading to the back room, firing his own gun. His first shot was intended for Cashman, but it missed wide. As he aimed for a second shot, Cashman had pulled his own rifle up and aimed it at his assailant. Other guns were being fired as general mayhem broke out, but to Cashman and the constable, only two people existed in the room, and they each had a bead drawn on the other.

CHAPTER I

Salem, Massachusetts, 1880

Mark Twain once described London as a city of villages. In reality, many American cities became cities of villages as immigrants from different parts of Europe created ethnic neighborhoods by choosing to live in areas where their fellow countrymen lived. Salem, Massachusetts, was one of these cities, and the Irish section was on the north end of the harbor. Irish immigrants had populated this part of the city. Their numbers increased dramatically during the period from 1845–1855.

Derby Street ran along the Salem Harbor waterfront and was the main thoroughfare of the Irish section of the city. The views of Salem Harbor were beautiful, but it was a poor section of the city. Salem was a city with a rich heritage and a good number of historical landmarks. Derby Street was home to one of the most famous of those landmarks— Nathaniel Hawthorne's House of Seven Gables.

On this October evening, John H. McCarthy was interested in a different Derby Street landmark, Timmy O'Shea's pub. As he made his way from his home on Blaney Street to the pub, he was greeted by a number of friends in this close-knit Irish community, and the salt air and pleasant fall night were comfortable and relaxing. His ultimate destination would be anything but. He was headed to O'Shea's as the main attraction in tonight's fight card.

O'Shea's was the most popular neighborhood tavern in this section of town, a true gathering place for the clan. Irish Heritage Club meetings were held on the second floor, and the bar on the first floor was warm and inviting in spite of its large size. The second floor also played host a couple of times a month to prizefights held using the bare-knuckled London Prize Ring Rule. Such events were against the law, but police in the district tended to look the other way, and precautions were taken to keep them from gaining access to the bouts in case an unfriendly constable should happen to have the beat on the night of a fight.

On this particular night, McCarthy was on the program for his fourth fight of this type. Although slight in stature, he had always demonstrated athletic ability and a competitive nature in sports. He held a record of two wins and one defeat. Tonight he would face Peter Dwelly, a more experienced fighter from nearby Swampscott. The price of admission to the second floor for these events was two dollars, and the crowd it attracted was made up of gamblers for the most part. The gate was split up one half to the house and a quarter each to the combatants. With the ring taking up a good chunk of space, the facility, while large, would only hold a crowd of sixty or seventy spectators, meaning McCarthy could expect a purse of thirty to thirty-five dollars, which was more than he makes for a week's work at a local cigar manufacturer, Battis and Brown.

Upon entering the tavern, Jack (as John H. is known to everyone) was greeted with handshakes and slaps on the back from the regulars who were all aware that he was on tonight's fight card. The tavern was large with a healthy seating capacity and a forty-foot bar. Behind the bar was a partially concealed rope that when pulled signaled the crew behind the upstairs bar that an unfriendly constable had entered and the fight needed to stop. A rather burly employee collected the cover charge and basically guarded the stairway to the second floor.

Jack's best friend and coworker, Peter Grady, was waiting near the stairs for Jack. Peter was the son of Henry Grady who, just like Jack's father, came to America to escape the famine. Peter would be active as his second, working his corner. The room was blue with smoke, but Jack saw him. He waved Jack over to a table, and they sat to discuss the fight in the thirty minutes they had until fight time.

Jack asked, "Is my opponent here?"

"He is, and I would guess he comes in ten or fifteen pounds heavier than you. He has a tough, hard look to himself."

Jack McCarthy stood 5'8" tall and weighed 160 pounds. He had a hard wiry build, and he was strong for his size, but the weight difference was troubling.

"Did he come with an entourage or by himself?" Jack asked.

"He has three guys with him, and I would guess the total brainpower might equal one normal man. They were all knuckle draggers. He even brought his girlfriend. She's right over there at the end of the bar. I guess she doesn't want to see the fight."

"Good God, Peter, as my mother would say, she has a face like a hen's ass on a frosty morning trying to lay an egg."

The two shared a laugh at this description, then Jack got serious.

"This whole thing doesn't sound good. We better head upstairs so I can get a look for myself."

"You still have time to make a run for it, Jack," Peter offered with a broad smile. Jack answered with a dirty look and a one-finger salute.

The noise level on the second floor was deafening as gamblers placed their bets in between shots of whiskey at the bar. Jack looked around for his opponent and found him shadowboxing near the ring, surrounded by his entourage. He was indeed noticeably bigger than Jack, and worse, his movements were graceful, and his hand speed was impressive. He was a good three inches taller, and Peter may have been underestimating the weight differential. Jack stood and spent some time examining his opponent. As he sized him up, he was sure he was in for a battle.

Jack's attention shifted to the bar where one man was attracting an inordinate amount of attention.

"Peter, look over at the bar. Is that who I think it is?"

"Yes, it is. I wanted you to be surprised. You're going to be fighting in the presence of John L. Sullivan."

"Saints preserve us, the Boston Strong Boy in Salem. Look at the size of him. He is as impressive as I have heard."

John L. Sullivan was not yet recognized as the heavyweight champion of the world, but his reputation in greater Boston had already been made. He had a number of victories under his belt and was gaining a national reputation among fans of the "sweet science." Jack had heard the story of Sullivan walking into the famous Harry Hills Dance Hall and Boxing Emporium on New York's east side and offering fifty dollars to anyone who could go four rounds with him. Several tried, but none succeeded. At 5'10" and 195 solid pounds, he was an imposing figure, and he immediately impressed the nineteen-year-old John H. McCarthy.

"Well, Peter, his presence will give me all the more incentive to win."

"I don't want to disappoint you, Jack old friend, but I think he is betting on Dwelly."

Jack shot him a look and responded, "Well, I'm going to cost the Boston Strong Boy some money."

THE FIGHT

In London Prize Ring rules for bare-knuckle boxing, a round ended when one fighter was knocked down or got to his knees. That fighter then had thirty seconds in his corner to recover, and eight more seconds to get to the center of the ring or the "scratch." The brutality of this type of prizefighting caused most states to ban it as a sporting activity. So even in this Irish neighborhood in which the local police had a tendency to "let boys be boys," precautions were taken, just in case. The fight could be stopped in a moment's notice if the signal was received from downstairs. The door at the top of the stairs was locked as soon as the fight began.

As this night's fight began, Dwelly and Jack circled one another, throwing jabs and feeling each other out. Both fighters had very quick hands, but in early clinches, it became obvious that the larger Dwelly had the strength advantage. Both fighters landed several blows on their opponent, with Jack's best shot a right hand that connected square on Dwelly's chin. The first round ended when Dwelly's second left-right combination of the round knocked Jack down. The right hand landed on Jack's cheekbone and put him on his knees.

Peter Grady helped Jack back to his corner on wobbly legs and toweled him down.

"Okay, Jack, we got thirty seconds. Shake it off."

"Shake it off? What the fuck did he hit me with?"

"Come on, man, you can handle this bloke. He punches like my sister."

"Remind me not to mess with your sister."

Jack was at the scratch for round 2 and round 3, which both went much like round 1. Jack did a little better job avoiding Dwelly, but in the end, he was flattened again by a Dwelly combination. This time, when he got back to his corner, Peter was joined by none other than John L. himself.

Sullivan leaned in and said, "Listen, kid, when he is going to throw that combination, he drops his left shoulder. If you duck away from the right cross, he leaves himself open for a left hook."

Jack listened to this advice from the great fighter in a daze, both from the punches and from the fact he was getting advice from John L. Sullivan. He nodded his head and walked to the scratch for round 4. Sullivan looked over at Peter Grady and gave him a wink.

For the first half minute of round 4, Jack stayed away from Dwelly and clinched whenever they were close. He was trying to clear his head enough to focus on Sullivan's advice. They sparred for a second full minute before Jack noticed Dwelly drop his left shoulder. The left hand punch grazed Jack's cheek and right ear, but he ducked the right cross altogether, coming up from the crouch to land a blistering left hook that staggered Dwelly for the first time in the fight. He tried to press the advantage with a combination of his own, but Dwelly was able to slip the right-hand punch. Then Dwelly once again dropped his left shoulder and repeated the combination move. Jack again avoided the right and landed another solid left hook that put Dwelly on his knees and ended the round.

The locals in the crowd cheered loudly as Jack won his first round. Jack walked back to his corner. He looked over at Sullivan, who raised his whiskey glass and gave him a wink. Jack smiled and pumped his right fist.

Round 5 began with the two fighters feeling each other out again as in round 1. Jack was feeling new confidence knowing that he had Dwelly's combination move figured out. About one minute into the round Dwelly, a right-hander, suddenly shifted to leading with his right. He aggressively backed Jack up with a series of right-handed jabs putting him on his heels. He then stepped into Jack and threw a vicious straight left hand that landed smack on Jack's face. The impact of the blow could be heard over the din of the crowd and actually brought the room to silence as Jack hit the floor. Peter entered the ring to bring Jack to his corner, but he was out cold, and the fight was over. It took Peter more than the allowed thirty seconds just to get Jack back to the corner, still unconscious. As the fight was ruled over, Peter had a couple of locals help him lay Jack out on a table.

When he woke up, the second floor crowd had thinned out as he had been laid out atop a table. Several people came into view as he opened his eyes. Peter Grady was there, of course, but standing next to him was Sullivan himself.

"How you feeling, champ?" Sullivan said with a smile.

"I guess I will live, but I won't be happy, and I probably won't live well."

"Well, he caught you with a good one. You had never seen a right-handed fighter lead with his right before, I take it."

"You take it right, and I don't want to see it again."

Jack sat himself up and tried to shake out the cobwebs. His head was splitting, and his entire face felt swollen and sore.

"Where did Dwelly go? I'm ready for round 6," he said, bringing laughs all around.

Peter answered, "I think by now he's halfway back to Swampscott. The real bad news is, he broke your nose again, and your Ma's probably going to break your ass when she sees it."

Jack tenderly touched his swollen nose and felt the bandage holding it in place.

"Mr. Sullivan here set it back in place while you were out, but the swelling has gotten steadily worse."

Jack looked at Sullivan, "Thanks, Mr. Sullivan, but the beating I just took will be nothing compared to the one I will take from my ma. She does not like me fighting, and she has a better right cross than Dwelly."

Jack's mother Johanna was a tough take-no-bullshit Irishwoman. Widowed quite young with two small children, she had a long history of taking care of herself, and she could put the fear of God in you with a look.

"Well, son, I have to tell you after watching you in action, I don't blame her a bit." This Sullivan comment also drew laughter, and he followed with an invitation to go downstairs and have a drink. "I will buy the first round with the money I won betting on Dwelly." More laughter at Jack's expense.

John L. Sullivan was born October 15, 1858, in South Boston to Irish immigrant parents. By the time he sat down with Jack McCarthy for a drink in Timmy O'Shea's, he had established himself as an outstanding prizefighter whose reputation went beyond greater Boston. To Jack McCarthy, it was an opportunity to have a conversation with a true rising star and, perhaps, more importantly, with a fellow Irishman.

They sat at a table, Sullivan, Jack, and Peter Grady. Peter went to the bar and brought back three beers and three shots of whiskey. Jack had a splitting headache, and his broken nose continued to swell, but he was not going to pass up an opportunity to sit and talk with the most famous Irishman in America.

"So," Sullivan said as he downed the shot and took a drink from his beer, "tell me about yourself."

"Not that much to tell, son of Irish immigrants, I live on Blaney Street about four blocks from here with my mother and older brother, Tom. I started fighting to earn a little extra money because I work for a cigar manufacturer, and the pay is not great."

"Where is your father?"

"My father died in a cart accident when my mother was pregnant for me."

"Your parents came over during the famine, I imagine, just like mine. Where in Ireland did they come from?"

"My father, John McCarthy, was from Skibereen, and my mother, Joanna Cashman, was from County Cork, a small town outside Cork City called Killy Donoghue."

"And your mother doesn't want you fighting. I have to tell you, if you want to stay in the prizefighting business, you need a lot of training. I'm not sure it's for you."

"After tonight, neither am I. What about you? Your family can't be too happy about you being arrested for prizefighting."

"How did you know that?"

"Read it in the Boston paper."

Sullivan laughed. "The press is not always good. My Da wanted me to be a priest, so I enrolled at Boston College. After a few months there, I turned to professional baseball for the money. Then I found out I could make more money as a prizefighter."

"I would like to see you fight. I've heard so many stories, it would be great to see you in action."

"Why don't you join me in Boston when I line up my next sparring session? You can be in my corner."

The offer obviously excited Jack. The prospect of working with this great fighter was overwhelming. He could not believe he was having this conversation. Sullivan had made arrangements to spend the night at the Hawthorn Hotel, which was only a few blocks away. So he was in no hurry to end the night.

They drank together as the night wore on, sharing stories with Sullivan gradually drawing more of a crowd around him to listen to his tales. As they parted company later that night, it was clear that Sullivan had taken a liking to Jack and that Jack had made a friend. He did not have any idea as yet what an impact that friendship would have on his life or the lives of his family.

CHAPTER II

Jack McCarthy's parents came to America to escape the Irish famine. They were among the nearly two million that left the country. Sadly, over one million that stayed died of hunger. To fully understand the degree and the intensity of the Irish resentment of the British, one needs to understand the devastation of the famine. The famine was caused by a blight on the potato crop that had spread through Europe. The scientific name for the blight is *Phytophthora Infestans*, and it was particularly devastating to Ireland for a couple of reasons.

First, Ireland's climate of continuous rain and high winds spread the fungus rapidly. It lasted season after season for seven years from 1846–1852. Second, the culture of the country at the time resulted in the impoverished class of bound tenant farmers, called cottiers, who existed primarily on the potato crop being left with nothing on which to survive. These tenant farmers worked as laborers for the wealthy landowners and were paid by being allowed to grow potatoes for the tenant farmers' families on small tracts of land. The potato crop they grew was the primary and often the sole form of nourishment for their family.

Fully three-fourths of the cultivatable land in Ireland was in other crops than potatoes. Grains, wheat, oat, barley, and vegetables were all grown on the three quarters and plentiful during the famine years. The cottiers and farm laborers were forced to subsist on what they could grow on the remaining one quarter. This group made up roughly six million of Ireland's eight million people. Three quarters of the population forced to exist on one quarter of the cultivatable land. Given these facts, the potato was the only crop that could sustain them. Their hand-to-mouth existence left no room for error.

When the blight hit, the fungus that came from the ground caused the potatoes they dug to turn into a blackened mess of slime that went to mush in their hands.

During the entire seven-year blight, other crops grown in the country were unaffected. Indeed, food exports including meat, grain, and vegetables increased while tens of thousands of impoverished Irish families starved to death. To the shame of the British, much of the food products exported from Ireland found their way to dinner tables in Britain while the *laissez-faire* attitude of their government left Irish families starving while Britain took no action.

In the winter of 1846–47 alone seventeen million pounds sterling worth of grain, cattle, pigs, flour, eggs, and poultry were shipped to England while four hundred thousand people were dying of famine-related diseases. More than enough food left Ireland to feed the six million men, women, and children classified as tenant farmers for the entire year.

A half million Irish tenant farmers were evicted from their tiny plots of land and pitiful cottages during the seven years. Men, women, and children were dragged from their shanties that would then be destroyed. Unscrupulous landowners would either apply for legal judgments first and then serve eviction notice, or they would simply use small gangs made up of starving fellow Irish to evict the families and destroy their living quarters. In the more formal process of obtaining a judgment, first, the man would end up in jail, and then the wife and children would be dumped onto the street. In some cases, the landlord would actually pay to send the family to Canada, on what became known as coffin ships. It is estimated that one in five passengers on such vessels died from disease and malnutrition in transit.

The starving peasants resorted to innovative use of what was left of their rotted crops. Partly rotted potatoes were reduced to pulp and made into "boxty" by squeezing out the water and flattening what was left to be cooked over coals. Resorting to eating whatever they could get their hands on to avoid starvation became the practice as many died with "green mouth," a condition caused by eating grass.

Death by starvation was often preceded by bruise-like spots on the skin, gums turning purple and ulcerated loss of teeth and hair, as well as festering sores emitting a putrid smell. Malnutrition brought on a variety of fevers, dysentery, famine dropsy, and typhus carried by lice and vermin. The emaciated blank stares of the children as they suffered the effects of the starvation that killed them were often the last things the parents saw.

All this was happening in a country that existed at the time under the protection and dominion of Great Britain. Rather than give assistance or feel any responsibility in England, the press, as well as comments made in Parliament, blamed the plight of the peasants on their own laziness and inability to help themselves. Absent any assistance from Great Britain, eventually other countries, most notably the United States, sent food to help alleviate the starvation. The British, never missing an opportunity to make money off other people's suffering, insisted that any foreign assistance must be delivered on British vessels.

Jack McCarthy's family lived in Skibereen, a Cork County town particularly hard hit by the famine. His grandfather Mike was one of the bound tenant farmers or cottiers, as they were known. As the famine hit in 1847, Mike, sensing that this was not going to be a one-season event, decided to begin sending his five children to America. His oldest son, John, would be the first to go.

Mike's sister worked in Cork City as a cleaning woman for a number of the wealthier Cork City merchants. John was dispatched to the city to work for his Aunt Pauline, doing the heavier chores in order to earn enough money to buy passage on one of the many ships that sailed from Cobh Harbor, which was just outside of Cork City. The plan was to have one of the five children follow this path until they were all safe in America. The first to go would send money to help those who followed.

The plan worked for Jack's father, John, and he secured passage on the Nautilus and arrived in Boston in 1849. The second child, James, sailed from Cobh that same year but died of malnutrition halfway over and was buried at sea. That very same year, Mike, his wife, Eileen, and the three remaining children were thrown out of their cottage and left to the street. As far as John ever knew, they all died of starvation. Neither John nor any of the members of his family could read or write. They never knew how John made out, and he never knew for certain what happened to them. Jack would find out later.

On the Nautilus, John met his future wife, Johanna Cashman, who was also escaping the famine. Johanna's family lived in the outskirts of Cork City in an area known as Killy Donoghue and fared far better than the McCarthys in dealing with the famine. The Cork City area was not hit nearly as hard as Skibereen, and the Cashmans, while being tenant farmers like the McCarthys, were able to hang on through the famine years. This was partly because Cork was not hit as hard by the blight and partly because the landowner they worked for was generous enough to grace the family's dinner table with vegetables other than potatoes that were grown in their field.

Still, even with these factors, the Cashmans sent two of their four children to America, Johanna and her brother Patrick. Patrick, a strapping 5'9" and 175 pounds, settled in Boston upon his arrival in 1849 at nineteen years of age. He began work as a laborer in the construction industry and by 1860 had started his own company, which prospered and grew rapidly in South Boston. Johanna moved to Salem and married John McCarthy in the Immaculate Conception Church in 1855. Unlike many Irish immigrants, she was educated enough to be able to read and write and was somewhat refined. Johanna was an attractive woman standing 5'4" with light-brown hair and blue eyes. John McCarthy stood 5'8" with a slight build. Together they had two children—Thomas, born in 1857, and John H. John died in a cart accident while Johanna was pregnant for their second son in 1860. Johanna was left a widow with two small boys.

The famine years and what they did to Irish families created bitter feelings toward the British. Jack's best friend Peter Grady was equally angry. His family came from County Kilkenny and was completely wiped out by the famine, with the members either leaving Ireland or starving.

Growing up in Salem, Jack heard the stories of the famine years and knew full well that the inaction of the British made the suffering of the Irish people and his very family far worse than it had to be. Both he and Peter Grady read accounts of speeches on the floor of Parliament where British MPs called the Irish less than human and the cause of their own troubles. His Uncle Patrick regaled them with many stories from home and introduced them to a number of Fenians that escaped to Boston after their 1867 Fenian uprising was crushed. The famine hardened resentment toward the British that led to the Fenian rebellion and the subsequent movements for home rule in Ireland. It was the direct cause of the formation of the Irish Republican Brotherhood and its American counterpart, the Fenian Brotherhood. These groups went beyond a call for home rule and pushed for complete independence. These movements now had a powerful new component of sympathetic Irish immigrants living in America. Many of the immigrants, like Patrick Cashman, had prospered in America in spite of the "Irish need not apply" signs. Through his Uncle Patrick and his friendship with John L., Jack would be meeting a good number of well-to-do Irish Americans who sympathized with the cause back home, and this would have a tremendous impact on Jack's life and on the life of his best friend, Peter Grady.

CHAPTER III

His family's past and the past of the Irish people in general, their dealings with the British, and Jack McCarthy's future associations would prove to shape his attitude about Ireland and the British. However, for now, his main concern centered on approaching the breakfast table and the wrath of his mother. The cottage at 6 Blaney Street was very small with only three rooms. One bedroom for Johanna and one for Jack and Tom. A common room served as kitchen and living room. The building was quite rundown and leaned towards the bay. It was badly in need of paint, and the roof leaked. It was all John and Johanna could afford, and they had rented it for twenty five years. John and Johanna had moved in the day they were married.

At the end of Blaney Street, a leather factory operated right on Salem Harbor. It was a noisy and smelly neighbor standing next door to the McCarthy home. On the other side, a triple-decker building was home to two other Irish families of related brothers.

Jack came to the kitchen at his home to join his mother, Johanna, and his brother, Tom, for breakfast. Sunday mornings at 6 Blaney Street meant breakfast followed by a walk to the Immaculate Conception Church for Sunday mass. In each of the Catholic ethnic neighborhoods, there stood a Catholic church for that ethnic group. The Immaculate Conception was the city's Irish church. Johanna came from a strong religious background and instilled it in her sons. Both Jack and Tom had served as altar boys in their youth. Johanna insisted on church attendance, and she said a rosary every night.

As he walked in the kitchen, he knew that when Johanna saw the condition of his nose he was in for a lecture. Years of hard living had robbed Johanna of much of her youthful beauty, but she was still an imposing figure as she moved through her fifties. She was in the process of cooking breakfast, wearing her best Sunday dress. She only owned three, and they were all well-worn and, of course, full length.

"Well, just look at the face on him. I've seen better looking faces on farm animals" was her opening salvo. He now had two black eyes to complement the swollen nose.

"You went in the ring again and got yourself busted up for what? A lousy few dollars. You came home with a broken nose and broke your mother's heart." She finished the statement shaking her head in disgust.

"Ma, it's not as bad as it looks. I'll be fine in a few days."

"Prizefighting is a sport for fools, Jack. If your father was here, he would tell you the same thing." She had her hands on her hips and a mean look on her normally sweet face that scared Jack far more than anyone he might face in the ring. She had always been able to put the fear of God into her sons when she gave them that same look.

Tom chimed in. "It's only a harmless hobby, Ma. He won't be doing it forever. Besides, he has his eye on Anna Hennessey, and she won't be looking at him long with a face like that."

This brought a menacing stare from Jack to his older brother and a look from his mother that said "Mind your own business." Tom put his head down, thinking he should do just that.

"Tom, you wouldn't look that bad if all the belts in the leather factory let go at once and smacked you in the face."

"Okay, Ma, enough. Last night was my last time in the ring." Jack said announcing a decision he had come to the night before.

"Jack, you look me in the eye and promise me that, and remember, we are headed to church, so don't lie."

He knew better than to lie to his mother for a couple of reasons. First, she had a sixth sense for smelling them out. Second, when his actions later proved the statement to be a lie, the consequences could be severe.

"I promise. I'm all done," he repeated as he looked his mother in the eye.

Johanna held her stare in to Jack's eyes for a full ten seconds then nodded her head as to say "Okay, it's done." As she went back to preparing breakfast, Jack told his brother, Tom, about John L. Sullivan setting his broken nose and inviting him to a sparring session in Boston. While not a pugilist or even a big fan of prizefighting, Tom was suitably impressed to hear that his little brother had met the great John L.

"I tell you, Tom, he is the most impressive man I have ever met. A huge man with thick muscle, arms like tree trunks. You would have to be a fool to enter the ring with him."

"What on earth was he doing at Tim O'Shea's?"

"He came up to see my opponent fight. He had heard of him and wanted to see him in action."

"By the look of you, he lived up to his reputation."

"Very funny. Sullivan even had money on him."

"So why did he end up drinking with you and Grady?"

"Because he's Irish. He may have been more impressed with Dwelly as a prizefighter, but Dwelly is not Irish like McCarthy."

"If you go to see him spar or just go to Boston to meet him, bring me along."

As she fixed oatmeal, soda bread, and tea for the three of them, Johanna listened to her sons' conversation and was not impressed.

"Now, Tom," interjected Johanna, "don't you start setting your sights on this sport for fools."

"Not to worry, Ma. I would just like to meet John L. Sullivan, and I bet Uncle Patrick would like that too."

Johanna just shook her head and served the breakfast the three ate in silence. She was well aware of Sullivan's fame but unimpressed at how he obtained it. Still she knew Tom was right, that her brother would jump at the chance to meet him. After finishing breakfast, the three would head to church. Their journey would bring them first to the corner of Blaney and Derby Streets.

The double-decker home at Four Blaney, on the corner of Blaney and Derby Streets, housed two families of Hennesseys. Anastasia Hennessey was the sixteen-year-old daughter of Mike Hennessey, the second brother to come over from Ireland. Mike's brother, Bill, came over in the famine years and was well established in Salem by the time his brother joined him in 1866. Anastasia was born in Kilkenny and came to America with her family as a small child. She had grown up next door to the McCarthys, so she and her sister Bridget, who was fifteen months older than Anna, had spent years playing with Jack and Tom along the Salem waterfront. She was coming out of her house to head to church when she saw the McCarthys headed her way. The first thing that caught her eye was the broken face of her friend Jack. At sixteen years of age, she had come to regard Jack as more than a next door playmate. He was a handsome young man with bright blue eyes and an engaging personality. She had picked up the impression that he felt attracted to her, but he was basically shy so he had never openly expressed any such feelings.

"Saints preserve us, Jack, what has happened to your face? You look as if the roof fell in on you."

Jack broke into a smile and answered, "I had a rough night at Tim's pub last night."

"You got back into the prizefighting ring. Mrs. McCarthy, I thought we had steered him away from any further fighting." She looked over at Johanna for support. As she spoke, she adopted the same hands-on-hips pose as Johanna. At 5'3" and 110 pounds, she was not nearly as intimidating, but she had a beautiful face and a smile that melted Jack like butter on a hot day. Her auburn hair and green eyes completed the Irish beauty that she had grown to be.

"He has promised me this very morn that he is done with it, and I'll be looking for help from you, Anna, to see to it that he keeps his word." Both women then looked at Jack for confirmation that his prizefighting days were indeed over.

'You'll stand no chance, Jack, fighting the two of them," said Tom. "I think you will come out looking even worse than you do right now." A broad grin was on his face as he spoke these words.

Jack just shrugged his shoulders and said, "I know when I'm licked. They'll not be seeing me in the ring again, I promise both of you."

Anna looked over at Johanna, and they nodded at each other, signaling that the issue was closed. With that, they all started up Derby Street headed to Sunday mass.

As Anastasia had reached her midteens, she had developed a figure to go with her beauty, and this figure had not escaped the attention of Jack McCarthy, and Jack's growing fondness had not escaped the attention of his older brother, Tom. Likewise, Anna's sister Bridget was well aware of the mutual feelings between the two. She encouraged her sister to let the relationship take its course. She liked Jack a lot and felt he was good for Anna.

As the three McCarthys left their cottage for the walk up Derby Street to the church, Anna was joined by the rest of the Hennesseys to begin the same walk. Bridget and Anna talking back and forth and smiling at one another made Jack a bit uneasy that they were talking about him, which they were. His brother found his unease amusing.

As they entered the church, the McCarthys moved into a pew first. Bridget guided Anna into the same pew, making sure she sat next to Jack. After brief prayers, they all took their seats, with Bridget quite pleased with her arrangement. The seating was not quite as pleasing to Johanna or to Mike Hennessey, who both kept a scornful eye on the two.

After mass, Jack and Tom walked back up Derby Street with Anna and Bridget well ahead of the rest of the pack. Johanna walked with Anna's parents. There was plenty of social interaction in both groups. Jack and Anna were both enjoying each other's company. They spoke back and forth about Jack's ill-fated fighting career, with Jack pointing out his good fortune in meeting John L. Sullivan. Even the Hennessey sisters had heard of him and were impressed that Jack had met him. Still, the two girls could not help teasing him, saying that by the look of him, Sullivan was probably not as impressed with Jack as he might have been with Sullivan. Tom joined in the good-natured ribbing of his brother. Jack took it all in stride. He was pleased with anything that made Anna smile.

CHAPTER IV

Jack's friendship with John L. Sullivan developed over the winter months. Several trips into Boston were taken on weekends either to see him spar or just to get together in Southie and do a bit of bar hopping. Jack was a bit cautious at first. He wasn't sure if the most popular Irishman in the country really wanted to be his friend or if the initial meeting was just a guy with a good personality being friendly. He was careful not to be a pest until he made his own determination one way or the other. After a couple of get-togethers, one that resulted in an all-night drinking session, he decided that the two of them had actually hit it off. What's more, they were often joined by Tom and/or Peter Grady, and Sullivan seemed to enjoy all their company. On several occasions, the bar hopping also included Jack's cousins, Jim and John Cashman, Pat's sons. They all enjoyed the company of John L., and he enjoyed them as well.

Sullivan introduced Jack to Pat McGowan, South Boston's leading real estate investor. Like many Irish, McGowan came to America in the famine years, and through hard work and smart investing, he had managed over thirty years to build up an impressive portfolio in real estate holdings and a strong cash position. It was well-known that McGowan took a keen interest in what was going on in his home country. He had lost family members during the famine and held very bitter feelings toward the British. It was rumored that he had sent financial help to the Irish Republican Brotherhood during the planning of the 1867 Fenian uprising. He continued to have involvement with groups in Ireland that were pushing for home rule and independence. He was not alone in this. A number of Irish immigrants in America, particularly in Boston and New York, had been successful in their new country and shared the same feelings toward their homeland. The Fenian Brotherhood was formed so that Irishmen from abroad could support the efforts of the Irish Republican Brotherhood. Fenian organizations had been established in Australia and Canada as well as the United States. The organizations in New York and Boston were particularly active. The Fenian Brotherhood held two key principles: first, that Ireland had a right to independence, and second, that that right could only be won by armed revolution.

Because Jack's uncle, Pat Cashman had started his own construction company and had a fair amount of success himself, it was natural that he and Pat McGowan should meet. On a trip into Boston in early February, Jack brought his brother, Tom, in with him for a couple of reasons. One was to meet with Sullivan and McGowan and introduce his Uncle Pat to the two of them. Second, he and Tom had made arrangements to rent a building on the corner of Becket and Derby Streets, and they intended to open a store and lunch counter. They were looking to borrow the start-up money from their Uncle Pat.

Pat lived in a very nice two-story home in South Boston with his wife, Barbara, and three sons and one daughter. Two of his sons, James and John, were close to the ages of Jack and Tom. Growing up, the McCarthy brothers had spent a good deal of time with their uncle and cousins in summer months. Pat, being so much better off financially than his widowed sister, insisted on taking the boys off her hands for long stretches in the summer months. This was the only form of assistance that the very proud Johanna would accept. Pat's daughter, Dierdre, was a year older than Jack, as she and the two older boys were all born within a four-year span. The youngest son, Conor, was referred to by Pat as the "family surprise." At age five, he was a late and unexpected addition to the Cashman family.

Jack had been working for the past two years for a local cigar manufacturer, Battis and Brown, and Tom had been working for three years at the leather factory next to the house at 6 Blaney Street. They had jointly reached the decision that they should start their own business. Two very popular brothers in a close-knit Irish community should do well with their own store. All they needed was some start-up money, and Uncle Pat was in a financial position to help. They would not be looking for a handout, so the two of them had worked out a plan for repayment that they felt could not fail.

Jack and Tom took the train in from Salem and arrived at their uncle's house in the early afternoon. Their goal was to borrow one thousand five hundred dollars, a considerable amount in 1881. They had saved money of their own but would need this loan to provide for working capital and stock for their grand opening. Both Jack and Tom had excelled in academics while going through the Salem school system, but this was their first attempt at drawing up a business plan. Pat looked over their proposed operating plan and was impressed that two inexperienced young men had put together a pretty good plan.

"You boys have done a nice job in designing this plan," Pat said after reading it over. "So how long do you two anticipate it will take you to pay me back?"

Jack answered, "We are confident that we will have your money all paid back within three years."

"You understand that a lot of young men start a business with all the best intentions, work hard, and still don't make it a success. What's your plan if business is not as good as you anticipate?"

Again Jack answered, "We have considered that, Uncle Pat. If things don't work out, we will sell off the remaining inventory and give you the proceeds. Whatever balance is left, Tom and I will work for you for nothing until we work it off. If you want that in writing, we will give it to you. The key is whatever happens, you will get your money back."

"No need to put it in writing. You're good lads, and I trust you, and after all, we are all family. I'm just trying to make sure you know what you are getting into. What kind of a lease do you have?"

"No lease. The property is owned by Danny O'Neil, and I guess we feel that we can trust him to treat us squarely."

Dan O'Neil was well-known and well respected in the Derby Street community, and Pat shared the same opinion as his nephews. "I think Dan will be more than fair with you. I've known him a long time. He's a good Irish boy. I think you lads are a good risk, so I'm willing to lend you the money. Will Johanna be involved in helping the operation along?"

"Yea, she will be working at the lunch counter three or four hours a day."

"My sister did one hell of a job holding things together after your father died. I hope you are successful enough to take care of her. She was too proud to ever take any money from me."

Many of the immigrants that escaped from Ireland in the famine years, including Jack and Tom's father, could neither read nor write. After John's death, Johanna made a little money reading letters from Ireland and writing letters back home for her neighbors. In addition, she performed other tasks—cleaning, some work as a nanny, whatever was available. Her brother had offered on several occasions to help financially, but Johanna would always refuse.

Having settled the first issue for which they came to Boston, the two brothers and their uncle headed out to see John L. and Pat McGowan. Sullivan would be sparring with another local fighter in a makeshift training facility in the back of a warehouse owned by McGowan. Pat Cashman had actually done some work in a couple of McGowan's properties but had never actually met him. He was anxious for the meeting and appreciated the opportunity to enhance his relationship with McGowan.

When the three arrived at the warehouse, Sullivan was finishing up a sparring session in a makeshift ring. A small crowd of about two dozen locals had gathered to watch the action. Pat McGowan saw them enter and waved them over to where he was standing. Introductions were made all around, and they stood together to watch the match.

John L. Sullivan cut an impressive figure in the ring. There was no athlete at the time as impressive to watch in action. His thickly muscled 195-pound body moved with surprising agility. His hand speed and the impact of his punches were incomparable among other fighters. He had a crouching, charging style, and when he moved in on an opponent, he showed impressive strength also unmatched in the ring. He was obviously pulling his punches and basically toying with an overmatched opponent as he worked on his craft. His trainer, Bill Madden, was at ringside intently observing every move while talking to Sullivan, giving instruction.

As the match wound to a close, the gathering applauded in appreciation. Sullivan, with a big smile, bowed to the crowd and stepped out of the ring. He walked directly over to the McGowan crowd, shaking hands along the way.

"You're looking great in there, John," McGowan allowed by way of a greeting.

"Ah, just getting some exercise to make sure I'm in decent shape for the real thing. Jack, glad to see you made it."

Jack shook Sullivan's hand and pointed out that he was accompanied by his brother, Tom, whom Sullivan had met before, and his Uncle Pat, whom he had not met.

Pat extended his hand and said, "It's an honor to meet you, Mr. Sullivan, all of Boston sings your praises."

Sullivan laughed. "Everyone loves you when you're winning. I just have to make sure I keep winning."

"Nobody's going to beat you, Sully," McGowan added, "you're the best there is."

"Well, Pat, can you bring my friends down to the pub while the best there is cleans up a bit. I will join you all shortly."

With that, McGowan and the McCarthys and Cashman proceeded to leave the warehouse and head to Southies, the nearest neighborhood pub.

After some initial discussion of Sullivan's performance and his future as a pugilist, McGowan and Cashman got into the more serious subject of doing more business together. It was a natural business arrangement. Two Boston Irish, one successful in the real estate development business and the other in the contracting business. They hit if off immediately, and it was obvious the deal would be made and a business relationship established. Over the years, this initial meeting would prove to be immensely profitable for both their organizations. In addition, the subject of Ireland came up, and they shared the feeling that the homeland should indeed have home rule and eventually complete independence. McGowan pointed out that he had been supporting the cause financially, and Cashman stated that he was interested in also giving financial support. They agreed to discuss this in more detail at future meetings and that McGowan would introduce Cashman to a number of Boston Irish who shared their views. He suggested, and Pat agreed, that he should join McGowan at the next meeting of the Fenian Brotherhood. This entire discussion fed the already strong feelings toward Irish independence that Jack and Tom felt. They were both well versed on the famine and the lack of effort on behalf of the British. What's more, they were both well informed by their uncle on the "Irish need not apply" signs that greeted him and their father's arrival in America. As Sullivan walked in and joined the table, the topic turned back to prizefighting. McGowan opened things by saying he was sponsoring Sullivan in his upcoming fight in New York.

"John has agreed to fight John Flood in New York in May," McGowan said. "This is a big fight against a well-known, highly rated opponent, and it will go a long way towards establishing him as the greatest prizefighter in the country."

Jack said that he had heard of John Flood. "They call him the Bulls Head Terror. It should be a hell of a match."

Sullivan was smiling when he said, "Yeah, he's a tough guy, but he's going to be in trouble when he gets in the ring with me. The details are still being worked out, but it will definitely be in May and in New York. I'd like to have you all come to the event."

McGowan was already planning to attend, and Pat Cashman said he would plan to be there.

"I'd love to go, but my brother, Tom and I are just now opening a store. I don't know if I can get away."

"Ah, come on, Jack, it will just be a long weekend, and I would like you to be working my corner." The suggestion that Jack might work in Sullivan's corner was a stunning offer that caught everyone by surprise.

"You have to do this, Jack. I will take care of the store for a few days while you're away. This is an opportunity you can't pass on." Tom, ever the loyal brother, jumped immediately into Jack's corner.

Jack appreciated his brother's offer, and the thought of working in John L. Sullivan's corner during a major fight was something he dared not even dream about.

"Well, I can't be arguing with you all. Uncle Pat, maybe we can take the train together."

"I will let you all know the details as soon as they have been worked out. The final detail will be which hospital to send Flood to when I'm done with him."

The table broke into laughter at this comment, and another round of drinks was ordered. Jack and Tom ended up staying at Uncle Pat's house that night so that Johanna would not see the condition they were in. They sat up drinking and talking with their uncle and two cousins. They talked a lot about the mechanics of running a business. Pat had been running his own business for twenty years. He learned a lot of the pitfalls the hard way. He had brought his two sons, James and John, into the business and taken great pains to see to it that they knew how to handle all aspects of running the operation. All three of the Cashmans had advice for the McCarthy brothers so that they would not have to learn the hard way. Sunday morning, they went to Pat's church with his family because they did not want to face their mother with a hangover and not having attended Sunday mass. Pat promised to swear to his sister that they had attended mass.

CHAPTER V

Having secured the loan from their uncle, the two brothers spent the rest of February and early March stocking their new store and getting ready for a scheduled St. Patrick's Day grand opening. Jack would be celebrating his twentieth birthday on March 16, the day before the opening. The store would feature basic household needs, and lunches would be served daily. Baked goods from Johanna's kitchen and homemade root beer would be high-demand items, as would the Irish home brew potien that the brothers made from a Cashman family recipe they received from Uncle Pat. The sale of this high-alcohol-content brew was done quietly and illegally to only a select group of customers. It was made in the basement of the store and stored in the coal bin so that even Johanna was unaware of its presence. It was a low-volume but high-profit margin product. Its availability also had the advantage of dramatically increasing the popularity of the store.

Johanna's service in writing letters home for many in the neighborhood and the popularity of her two sons and the newness of the store all combined for a tremendously busy grand opening. Customers and people who stopped by just to wish the boys well flooded the store from its opening at nine until after the successful first lunch. The lunch hour attracted a good number of Tom's former coworkers at the leather factory as well as other neighborhood businesses. As the day wore on, the crowd migrated more to Tim O'Shea's pub to celebrate the Irish holiday, but not before the new McCarthy Brothers Store had registered a land office opening. Jack's favorite customer, Anna Hennessey, came in at four thirty, and Jack was thankful things had slowed down enough that he could sit and have a cup of tea with her. Anna had just finished her day's work as a file clerk and receptionist at the textile mill.

"So, Jack, has it been a busy day for you and Tom's new venture?"

"Even better than we anticipated. Ma's Irish stew and soda bread were huge hits. We sold out of both. She went home around two o'clock to do some cooking for tomorrow."

"You're very fortunate to have her helping you. Everyone loves your mother, and she's a great cook. The woman's touch might save this place from the ruin you and Tom could bring to it."

This brought a smile to both of their faces as Jack enjoyed Anna's sarcastic Irish wit. "Thanks for the confidence you seem to have in me. Perhaps in spite of your obvious misgivings, you would agree to accompany me to the social event this Saturday evening."

Jack had been interested in Anna for a good long time, but this was his first attempt at actually securing a date. The social was at the Immaculate Conception Church, which they both attended, and he felt it would be a safe bet that Anna would accept. She did accept with more enthusiasm than he anticipated.

"I would love to go with you Jack. It took you long enough to ask. I was beginning to think I would have to do the asking myself."

Anna stayed at the store until closing time at six o'clock. They sat together and talked as long as Jack was able but duty called and took him away from time to time. Jack walked with her the short distance to her door, which was just across Derby Street, and having bid her good night, decided he would join the crowd at Tim O'Shea's for a few drinks. As he walked down Derby Street, he felt that life could not be any better. The girl who had captured his fancy as he watched her mature had agreed to accompany him on Saturday. The first day of business at his new store was a success, and he was truly a friend of the Boston Strong Boy, the most popular Irishman in Massachusetts. He felt truly blessed as he headed for an evening of drink with his brother, Peter Grady, and whoever else joined him.

As Jack approached O'Shea's, Tom was coming out the front door looking like he was dragging himself along on tired legs. Looking up at Jack, he said, "I'm headed home, Jack. I'm worn-out."

"Oh, come on, Tom, just one or two more with me."

"Your pal Grady is in there to keep you company. I'm beat."

Jack shook his head, called his brother a slacker, and went inside. He spied his friend Peter across the room sitting with two other locals. Looking up and seeing Jack, Peter got up with his drink and waved Jack over to an empty table. Jack motioned that he would grab a drink at the bar and then join him at the table.

As they sat down together, Peter was bursting with excitement, "Jack, I was in Boston last night and attended my first meeting of the Fenian Brotherhood. I tell you the best thing you ever did was introduce me to Pat McGowan and the other members of the group. I have taken the pledge." Peter raised his glass for a toast as he spoke.

Peter had joined in on a couple of trips into Boston, and he was enthralled with the stories of the Fenian Brotherhood and the efforts of Irishmen in America helping the Republican Brotherhood in the old country. Like many others, he had a number of relatives who starved during the famine and, of course, his father, Henry, had escaped the famine by coming to America. The bitterness against the British was difficult to wash away, and Peter held deep-seeded feelings and was enthusiastic about the prospect of helping in some small way to assist in gaining Irish independence. His membership in the Brotherhood was his first step in what would turn out to be his main focus in life.

"It is the most noble cause," Jack said as they clinked glasses. "I would like to join you in attending the next meeting you go to."

"Well, your Uncle Pat was there, and he is as dedicated to the cause as you and I."

"I know he joined the Brotherhood after meeting Pat McGowan, but he has always held strong feelings on the matter."

They spent the next several hours toasting the Brotherhood and the cause of independence. At eleven o'clock, Jack called it a night knowing he had another long day in the store tomorrow.

Things slowed a bit after the grand opening, but business remained steady. The brothers were pleased with the operation. Not only were they doing a brisk business, it was enjoyable to work there. The regulars were generally neighborhood friends, and the atmosphere was conducive to lively conversation and good-natured exchanges of both a serious and a joking nature.

Even as he worked, Jack could not get a certain customer out his mind. All week long, Jack looked forward to his date with Anna, and she dropped by the store at the end of each day for a cup of tea with Jack. They seemed to be getting closer, and Jack could not have been happier about it.

Saturday night rolled around, and sharply at six forty-five, Jack was knocking on the door of his neighbors. It was answered by Mike Hennessey, Anna's father. He and his wife were going to be at the same event, so he made sure Jack knew he would be keeping an eye on him. Anna had two brothers both younger than her and her sister, Bridget, who was slightly older. She and her sister were very close. They spent a good deal of time together, and Bridget also planned on attending the social. Anna's mother, Pauline, offered Jack some tea and cake, which Jack refused saying there would be plenty to eat at the church. With that, Jack and Anna headed out, and her parents said they would soon follow with Mike's brother, Bill, and his wife, Deirdre, who lived one floor below them.

Walking up Derby Street headed for the church, Anna said, "You know, my father really likes you, and he and my mother were glad you had asked me to go with you to the church social."

"What's not to like?" Jack asked.

"Do you want a list?" Anna replied. Jack could never get ahead of her.

"Well, we've been neighbors all my life, so I have always felt we got along. Even when we were young, and Tom and I used to tease you."

Jack reached over to hold Anna's hand and was surprised at the excited feeling that accompanied this simple contact. This was his first time dating. It was all the more special given the feelings he had developed for Anna. The simple gesture of holding her hand gave him goose bumps. He turned to look at her, and it was obvious to Anna that Jack had special feelings for her.

"I think your teasing days are over, Mr. McCarthy."

They smiled at each other as Jack answered, "I think you are right."

They walked up Derby Street holding hands and talking until they reached the Immaculate Conception Church. The church had activities on most Saturday nights, ranging from Beano to craft and bake good sales to socials. On this night, the social would include Irish music and refreshments provided by the parish women's group. There would be Irish step dancing by those who were able to step dance. Anna was included in the group that could, Jack in the group that could not. Jack sat on the sideline watching Anna's graceful movements as she joined in the step dancing.

The host on behalf of the church was a young priest, Father MacKenzie, whom they all liked, although Anna whispered that she thought he was built like a bag of doorknobs.

The evening went very well for Jack and Anna. They spent time with friends, enjoyed the food and entertainment, and mostly enjoyed being together. They walked home at ten when the social ended, holding hands as they did on the walk to the event. Arriving at 4 Blaney Street, they lingered for a moment in spite of the cold, making small talk and gazing into each other's eyes.

"You know, Jack McCarthy, I would not be offended if you kissed me goodnight."

Jack, being too shy to make the first move, appreciated Anna's invitation and leaned in for a kiss that was too short but filled with the most pleasurable exciting feeling he had ever experienced. They pulled back and looked at each other for a moment, and Jack said, "Anna, I would really like to do this again."

She smiled and answered, "You mean the kiss or the night together."

"Both," Jack said and kissed her again. They parted company for the evening, neither of them wanting to leave, but knowing that they would have to end their evening before Mike got home.

As March moved into April, the store and lunch counter gradually became one of the most popular gathering spots in the neighborhood. Jack found himself so busy the six days it was open that he was seeing less of his friend John L. The only free day he had was Sunday, and that day, along with a couple of weeknights, was time he could spend with Anna.

Uncle Pat came up a couple of times to see how things were going. On one trip, Sullivan came up with him, and the neighborhood was all abuzz with the excitement of having him there. When he walked into the store, he announced in a loud voice, "I can lick any man in the place." He made the statement with a broad smile that told everyone it was a good-natured greeting to let all know he was there. He continued to stress to Jack that he wanted him in his corner for the upcoming fight in New York. Uncle Pat was still intending to go with Jack, and Thomas was insistent that he could hold things together for a couple of days without Jack. Sullivan held court at the lunch counter for over an hour telling stories and arm-wrestling with a few of the locals. None could beat him. Jack snuck him a couple of shots of potien that he very much appreciated.

The fight date rolled around, and Jack and Pat headed down by train the day before. This was Jack's first trip to New York. He could not help but be amazed at the size of the city. They did some sight-seeing before fight day, and Jack was sure that New York must be the biggest city in the world.

On a bright sunny day on May 18, 1881, John L. Sullivan met John "The Bull's Head Terror" Flood in a prizefight. The combatants would be wearing "hard gloves" as opposed to bare knuckles, but the bout would be fought under London Prize Ring rules, meaning the rounds would end when a fighter went down. Such bouts were illegal in New York, so in order to avoid troubles with the law, the fight took place on a barge in the Hudson River.

Jack and Pat were on the barge along with a fair-sized crowd that included financial backers for each fighter and a good number of gamblers who had covered bets on the outcome. Bets continued to be made right up until fight time.

As Sullivan and Flood stood in the ring, they both looked ready for the match. Lean and hard and thickly muscled, they appeared to be a match for each other. As the fight started, it became clear early on that Sullivan was the superior combatant. Stronger, faster, and equipped with a powerful punch, Sullivan took charge from the start.

Round 1 ended with Sullivan landing a crushing right to the side of Flood's head that dropped him to the deck. Even after one round, Flood was noticeably wobbly going to his corner. He made it to the scratch in time for round 2, but he might just as well have stayed in his corner. Sullivan's right had left him dazed even after the thirty-second break.

After the knockdown that ended the fourth round, Sullivan came back to his corner and looked at Jack and said, "If you had brought some of you homemade potien, I could have drunk it in between rounds. This is such an easy fight." Jack told him not to get too confident until it was over. Sullivan just laughed.

The fight went four more rounds, and Flood hit the deck at the end of each of them. After the eighth knock-down ended the eighth round, everyone knew the fight was over. In spite of all the hype, Flood proved to be a less than worthy opponent for the Boston Strong Boy. Sullivan dominated from start to finish. The eight rounds was a far shorter fight than anyone had anticipated.

Jack had worked in Sullivan's corner, but it really did not involve any real work. He never went down and after round 3, was seldom hit with any force. His hands took more of a beating than the rest of his body. Besides, any real work that might have been needed would have been handled by his regular trainer, Bill Madden. Jack was there more as a friend than a professional. As he walked to his corner after round 8, Jack raised Sullivan's arm indicating the victor and the end of the bout. It was a bout that received national and some international press from reporters on the barge. It was not the first time the prizefight fans in the country heard of Sullivan, but it was to that date the fight that received the most coverage. It would turn out to be only the beginning of the fame and popularity of a great American sports hero.

Hours after the bout, as Jack and Pat joined the winner along with Pat McGowan, Bill Madden and others for drinks, Sullivan talked of his plans for the future. "I intend to take on all comers until I'm recognized as the prizefighting champion of the world. We are going to barn storm the country and take on all challengers. Jack, I would like you to come with me and work in my corner with Bill."

Jack was flattered and stunned at the proposal. It was indeed tempting to travel with a man whose potential seemed unlimited, to be part of a team that seemed destined for greatness. However, three thoughts came immediately to mind. The first was his obligation to his brother and his uncle to make a success of the store they opened. The second was the blossoming relationship with Anna Hennessey. Lastly, he felt an obligation to stay with his widowed mother. The early success of the store and Johanna's role in it had really lifted her spirits. The chance to work with her sons and actually make some money was a new and very enjoyable thing for her. It was truly a dream come true for a grand woman who had lived a very hard life.

"John, I couldn't be more flattered by your offer or more certain of your future success. But I have obligations back in Salem that I can't just leave to chance."

"If it's money that concerns you, I plan to make enough to pay the expenses for my entire traveling team. We have financial backers like Pat McGowan to make sure the finances are sound."

"It is not just that. I can't leave my brother and my mother with the sole responsibility for the business we started. Maybe I can meet you halfway, I'll attend some fights and work with you when you're in Boston. I don't think it's possible for me to travel the country with you. I just don't think it's possible." Left unsaid was Jack's desire not to stray too far from Anna.

"Well, at least give it some thought, Jack. I'd love to have you along."

Jack would end up not going along on the barnstorming tour, and he missed a real successful phase of Sullivan's career. Sullivan toured a number of cities taking on all challengers, thereby spreading his reputation as a great prizefighter. In addition, the tour raised by some estimates over a hundred thousand dollars, a tremendous amount of money for the times. It set him up in terms of his fighting career as well as his financial position. He visited a number of major cities on the tour from Cincinnati to Kansas City, St. Louis, New Orleans, Atlanta, and many others. He took on all that dared fight him and never lost.

As the night wore on and rounds of drink added up, Jack was not sure what had left a bigger impression, working the corner or having the offer to travel as part of the Sullivan team. It all seemed so implausible, and he found it hard to imagine that it all started with him getting beat up in Tim O'Shea's pub months ago. From that beating, he had struck up a friendship with John L. Sullivan and met South Boston's biggest real estate developer. He had made the connection with that developer for his Uncle Pat's construction company. McGowan had left the table with his Uncle Pat to introduce him to some of his friends in New York who were members of New York's Fenian Brotherhood and supported the Fenians back home in Ireland. McGowan also recommended Uncle Pat's company to his New York friends for any construction needs. It seemed that the ties to McGowan were pulling both Jack and his uncle more and more into the causes in their homeland. Given the history of the two, it may well have been inevitable.

CHAPTER VI

Upon his return to Salem, Jack settled into a routine that centered on the McCarthy Brothers' store and Anna Hennessey. Of course, the first few weeks involved telling and retelling the accounts of the great fight. It was the talk of greater Boston for weeks how Sullivan had made such short, relatively easy work of a highly regarded opponent. Of course, at the store, the bigger story was that Jack had worked in Sullivan's corner. He tried to be humble and downplayed his involvement, but to the Derby Street crowd, he was a local hero. Stories had been published about Sullivan's plan to barnstorm the country, and the locals wanted to know if Jack would be going. He answered these questions by pointing out that Salem was his home, and the store and his family were his first priority.

The store had quickly become a local hot spot for political discussions of all kinds, as well as the prizefighting discussions. Local issues around Salem City government were the most common topics, but state and national issues were not ignored. Neither were the issues in Ireland, with dated Irish newspapers being brought to the store after arriving from the homeland. The local Irish population would read and argue the issues just as if they were back in Ireland. The talk of events unfolding in Ireland always carried an undertone of British resentment. Virtually every family in this Irish neighborhood had a story of hardship in Ireland. Hardship made worse by British involvement.

It was a volatile time in Ireland with Charles Stewart Parnel pushing for a Home Rule Bill in Parliament. Meanwhile, the more radical Irish Republican Brotherhood saw home rule as only a first step. The ultimate goal needed to be complete independence, even if it took an armed insurrection to make it happen.

For Jack's part, he would join in all the debates and spend an occasional Sunday in Boston with his uncle, Pat McGowan, the Fenian Brotherhood, and other Bostonians who kept a keen eye on things back home. He was becoming more and more indoctrinated into issues of Irish Home Rule and the more aggressive push for Irish independence. Pat McGowan had given Jack a copy of the 1875 speech in New York by John O'Connor Power that spoke of the efforts to "offer unrelenting hostility to British rule." Jack shared the speech with Peter Grady, who loved it.

Peter Grady would often initiate discussions on such issues at the store. His enthusiasm for the cause was contagious, and many of the locals would leave the store almost as fired up as Peter.

Jack was also becoming more involved with Anna Hennessey. She accompanied Jack on a trip to Boston in July and shared Sunday dinner at Uncle Pat's with his wife, Barbara, his three sons, and his daughter. The Cashmans all took an instant liking to Anna and told Jack how lucky he was that she spent time with him. Her natural beauty and strong Irish wit were enough to win them over, but the kicker was her smile that would light up the whole room. Jack was invited to Sunday dinner with the Hennesseys on a somewhat regular basis, and all the Hennesseys from both families were regulars at the store. Jack and Anna spent more than a few nights during the summer sitting on her porch and looking out at Salem Harbor beyond the leather factory. His friends like Peter Grady were seeing less and less of him at Timmy O'Shea's as the McCarthy family was being more often represented by his brother, Tom. Jack had not only kept his promise to stay out of the ring, he was also staying out of O'Shea's altogether.

As 1881 turned into 1882, Jack was indeed a creature of habit. He had not seen Sullivan since the fight with Flood. There were newspaper articles in the Boston papers telling of his barnstorming, the take-on-all-comers tour around the US, but they had not had any contact with each other until Jack received a telegram on January 18 telling him that Sullivan wanted him to come to New Orleans to be in his corner for his big fight with Paddy Ryan. Jack was aware of the match, it having been announced in October of 1881. He was also aware of its importance. Paddy Ryan had declared himself to be the heavyweight champion of the world after he defeated Joe Gass in a brutal eighty-seven-round fight. His claim to the championship was supported by Richard L. Fox, owner of the popular *Police Gazette*, the primary publication for prizefight fans. The scheduled fight was getting more press coverage and promotion than any previous prizefight.

Jack would have loved nothing more than the opportunity to be there with Sullivan, his trainer Bill Madden, and Pat McGowan. The problem was that it was scheduled to take place so far away that he knew he would have to decline the offer and said so in a telegram to Sullivan, who was in New Orleans training. To miss the most important prizefight up to that time was disappointing, but New Orleans seemed like a world away to Jack. New Orleans had become the unofficial capital of prizefighting in spite of the fact that bouts held under the London Prize Ring Rules were still not legal there. This would be the most anticipated prizefight ever and would decide the heavyweight championship. Jack hated to miss it but knew he must.

The match took place without Jack's presence. Because of the legal issues, the match was moved out of New Orleans to Mississippi City. There in an oak grove in front of the Barnes Hotel, John L. Sullivan made short work of Ryan and all the *Police Gazette* hype. In nine rounds taking eleven minutes in front of five thousand people, he defeated Paddy Ryan with a final blow from his famous right hand, dropping Ryan in a heap. Sullivan walked out of the ring, recognized as the first undisputed heavyweight champion of the world and the winner-take-all purse in his pocket. The fight received international press reported in every major newspaper with coverage in some publications being reported by no less than Oscar Wilde. Sullivan was an international figure and a hero to the powerless and slighted Irish on both sides of the Atlantic. Jack could not have been happier for his friend who had become the first international sports hero ever. The name John L. Sullivan was known throughout America, Canada, and Europe.

When Sullivan returned to Boston, Jack went to see him with his brother and Peter Grady. A large group of supporters celebrated the great victory with the newly crowned champ. While the friendship between Jack and the champ would continue for the next few years, it would be limited to time spent together when Sullivan was in the Boston area. That would change in 1887.

The champ continued to fight anyone anywhere and offered money to anyone that dared enter the ring with him, and his fame continued to spread. Jack's commitment to the increasingly busy and profitable store was keeping him close to home. While he certainly had developed nothing like the fame of his friend, in his part of Salem, Massachusetts, he was becoming as well-liked and well respected as a local hero could be. More importantly, as far as he was concerned, he had won the heart of the most important person in his life. Anna Hennessey, the prettiest, wittiest girl in Salem, or any place else, was Jack McCarthy's girl. Of all the good fortune that he had been blessed with in recent years, this simple fact was the most important thing in his life.

CHAPTER VII

The four-year period from 1882 through 1886 saw a number of significant changes for the little family at 6 Blaney Street. McCarthy Brothers Store continued its success, and the brothers took over the lease to another section of the building and broke through the wall to expand their store in 1882. A larger variety of goods and a larger lunch counter increased the store's volume of business to the point that the brothers plus Johanna could no longer handle it alone. Tom had started seeing a young lady, Mary MacDonald, and she was hired to help with the increased business. In 1883, they were able to purchase the home behind the store on Becket Street and move into much better living quarters. The Becket Street home was two stories with three rooms on the first level and three bedrooms on the second, a marked improvement over the Blaney Street cottage. The humble cottage they had been renting for years at 6 Blaney Street was purchased by the adjacent leather factory and demolished.

Also in 1883, Jack asked Anna Hennessey's father for his blessing as he intended to propose to her. After giving Jack a bit of a tongue-in-cheek hard time, Mike Hennessey responded that he had been expecting the request and Jack could ask his daughter with his blessing. Having secured the family's approval, his next step was to talk with his mother. One night as the store closed at six, Thomas went off with Mary, and Jack went home, where he sat for dinner alone with Johanna.

"Ma, I have something important to discuss with you," he began. He was unsure of the reaction she would have to her twenty-two-year-old son leaving the nest. Since the death of her husband, Johanna had relied on her two boys for companionship and security as they got older. Now working with them on a daily basis, Jack was unsure exactly how dependent his fifty-eight-year-old mother had become on having her boys to herself. He knew she liked Anna very much but still would she look at this as adding a daughter or losing a son.

"Well, what can be so important that you send your brother off without supper?"

"I didn't send him off, Ma, he is seeing a good bit of Mary these days without any encouragement from the likes of me." At this, his mother smiled and looked across the table at her youngest son. She knew what was coming and felt a bit amused by the trepidation the telling was causing her boy.

Jack decided to just come right out with it. "I'm planning to ask Anna to marry me."

With only a moment's delay, Johanna shot back, "Well, it's high time you stopped taking up her time with no purpose." She smiled at her son who returned the look. "She is a beautiful young lady, Jack. You could hardly do better. Have you talked to Mike?"

"I have, Ma, and he approves."

"Well then, there's no time like the present. You've finished your dinner, so get up and get at it."

Jack stood and went over to his mother, who rose to greet him. They embraced for a long moment, and Jack allowed that he would be going over to the Hennesseys. Johanna pulled back from the embrace and looked at Jack, "It has been a hard life for us since your father's death. Things seem to have finally changed for the better with the store and all. It's like your father used to say, 'The luck you don't have today you might have tomorrow.' The good Lord is smiling on us, Jack. But none of that good fortune is as uplifting to me as the thought of you and Anna together."

Jack could not have hoped for a better response from his mother. He left feeling that he now had the full support of everyone, except the most important person, Anna.

It was a warm August evening as Jack was greeted at the upstairs apartment of the Hennesseys. He got the distinct impression that everyone in the house except Anna knew what he was up to. Her sister, Bridget, and her parents looked at Jack with broad grins on their faces. Anna came out, and Jack suggested a walk down Derby Street. As they walked along holding hands, Jack, who was obviously nervous, began the conversation. "You know, Anna, we have been seeing each other for a long time now."

"Yes, some would say too long." A cool and measured response.

That sarcastic sense of humor she had was one of her endearing qualities.

"Maybe, but I would like it to be longer." No response from Anna other than a smile, so Jack began to make his case. "The store has become quite a successful business, and I'm pretty well-established in terms of my future."

"Jack, I'm well aware of all that. If you are trying to tell me something, for the love of God, spit it out."

"I'm really trying to ask you something." He stopped and turned her to face him. "Anna, I want you to be my wife. Will you marry me?"

Anna looked in his eyes, smiled, and said, "Jack McCarthy, I would be more than happy to accept and proud to be your wife, but," she paused, "why are you not on your knee doing the asking?"

A silent moment then, as he broke into a wide grin, "Anna, is that a requirement in front of people out here on Derby Street?" Jack looked around at the busy street packed with people out for a walk on a warm night. Some people had stopped to watch the interaction between Jack and Anna. He looked back at Anna, and she nodded with a grin.

Jack dropped to one knee and repeated the question, and she laughingly accepted. The small group of onlookers that had stopped to watch as Jack dropped to one knee applauded their approval. They embraced right there on Derby Street, and both thought of their future while they relished a moment that they had both been anxiously anticipating.

They walked on to Tim O'Shea's, where Jack insisted on going inside. Once they were in, Jack hollered out to get everyone's attention. When the bar had quieted, he hollered out that he had "asked this beautiful lady to marry me, and she has accepted."

The crowd cheered and offered the couple drinks. Jack accepted congratulations from many friends and took one beer but left to go back to tell the Hennesseys and his family. Arriving back on Blaney Street at the Hennessey home, he and Anna joined a celebration with two Hennessey families as well as Johanna, Tom, and Mary.

Their Catholic religion required a series of instructions from their priest, as well as the banns of marriage being posted in the church bulletin three weeks in succession. Having this ahead of them, they planned a November wedding.

At the ceremony, Tom acted as best man, and the wedding drew a huge crowd from the neighborhood, as well as a crowd from Boston, including Uncle Pat and his family, Pat McGowan, and a number of other friends Jack had made on his many trips into Boston. The crowd also included the heavyweight champion of the world who came up with the crew from Boston. Jack had picked a date intentionally when he knew Sullivan was planning to be in town. There was nothing like having the most popular sports figure in the world at your wedding.

A reception followed the Christian wedding in the hall above Tim O'Shea's, where Jack had participated in his last prizefight. Tom offered a toast as the best man, followed by one from his good friend Peter Grady, and then by popular demand, a toast from John L.

"I congratulate this beautiful bride, Anna, and can only wish that Jack is a better husband than he is a prizefighter." Sullivan toasted to gales of laughter.

Anna's sister, Bridget, spoke about how long it took her to get the two of them together. It was a great event, with the happy couple receiving well-wishes from hundreds of friends and relatives.

The couple moved in with Tom and Johanna in the house on Becket Street behind the store. Anna continued to be employed at the Hamel & Barrows Textile mill as an office clerk, and Jack, of course, in the store.

In 1885 there were to be more successes and more changes in the lives of the McCarthys. In June of that year, Jack and Tom purchased the building they had been leasing from Danny O'Neil. They had started the store occupying half of the building. Then they expanded to taking over the entire building, so the next logical move was to buy the building. The purchase included the large apartment above the store. At the time of the purchase, the apartment had been vacant for two months, so Jack and Anna moved into it leaving the house to Tom and Johanna.

In December, Tom gave the family an early Christmas present by proposing marriage to Mary MacDonald. The two had been somewhat of an item for more than a year, and for a number of months, they had been working together in the store. It came as no surprise to Johanna, Jack, and Anna, but it was still a very well-received announcement. Mary was well-liked by all and a welcome addition to the family. Her family were longtime residents of the Irish section of town and steady customers at the store. Like most of the neighborhood, they had originally come to America in the famine years, worked hard, and raised their children here. Mary was a delightful hardworking Irish girl with a great cheerful personality. A June 1886 wedding was planned, after which Mary would move into the Becket Street house with Tom and Johanna.

Life was very good then on the corner of Derby and Becket Streets. The two brothers and their wives lived next door to each other and basically surrounded their store with their living quarters.

The loan from Uncle Pat had been paid off on time, and they owned the store and were in far better living quarters than they had at 6 Blaney Street. The store and lunch counter were more popular than ever, and Johanna was anxiously awaiting the arrival of grandchildren. Events were unfolding that would leave her waiting a while longer for Jack and Anna's firstborn.

John L. Sullivan was busy planning a trip to Ireland and Britain. The idea was for the champ to display his talents for his Irish countrymen to see and for him to take on the best prizefighters in Britain and beat them. He would be traveling with an entourage, and Jack was being recruited as part of that entourage.

Others had additional agenda items for the trip. Pat McGowan and a close friend, Dan Foley, were planning to go along to support Sullivan financially but also to have meetings with the principals involved in the Irish Republican Brotherhood and their push for independence. The purpose was to take stock of what they would need in Ireland and plan how the Irish in America could help provide it. Jack would, of course, love to visit the country and be part of the Sullivan entourage, but it was not that simple. A trip like this with all that was happening in their lives was far from simple.

Anna was anxious to get pregnant, and Jack had responsibilities both to his wife and to his business. This was far more than just a day trip to New York for a prizefight. He would be away for a considerable amount of time. His first step was to speak to Johanna, the person who had always been his first option for sound advice. Her advice for him was to get with his brother and his wife and talk the whole thing out. "Jack, I'm still able to step up and help your brother fill in the gaps. But you need to clear things with him. More importantly, you need to make sure your wife is all right with this."

"I plan to talk with Tom, Ma. I would not consider doing this without his blessing. The other thing I have decided is that if I go I would bring Anna with me."

"Have you discussed this with her, Jack? This is a big trip, and she has a lot to consider."

"I have told her that I've been asked to go along. She only shrugged in response, so I let it go."

"She has other considerations. What about her job?"

"Well, we are trying to have children, and when we do, she will have to quit her job anyway."

"Well, it seems to me that you have a good deal of talking ahead of you. You can thank the Lord that you are good at it."

He was indeed good at it. Jack had been blessed with ability to articulate his position on any issue, a quality that would serve him well in the future.

His discussion with Tom went better than he anticipated. He would be gone for two months, from late October to late December, assuming everything went well. Tom felt he and Mary and Johanna could handle things, and where there would not be any pay for Jack, they could afford to bring on some part-time help. Tom had another reason for wanting Jack to make the trip.

"Go, Jack, and find out what you can about what became of Da's family. We've been left in the dark about it all these years."

Jack shared Tom's feelings about solving the mystery of what happened to his father's family. This quest would be an important part of the trip. Their mother still had siblings living around Cork, but she had always refused her boys' request to ask them about their father's family. Johanna had felt it would be too painful to find out. Now, however, she agreed to write and ask them to see what they could find out in advance of Jack's arrival. Johanna's family back in Cork would do the best they could to unearth the facts of the disposition of John McCarthy's family.

Unlike Jack and Tom, Anna was born in Ireland in the town of Kilkenny. His approach to her was to try and make the trip out to be about her. "Anna, I have been thinking that this opportunity to travel to Ireland would be a chance for you to revisit the place of your birth and visit with some cousins," he began.

Anna looked quizzically at this and answered, "Jack, if that is your way of inviting me along on a trip you want to take, it's a bit clumsy. If you are going to try to outsmart someone, you have to begin by being smarter than the person you are trying to outsmart."

Again, that Irish sarcasm that, while always funny, was at times annoying. "Anna, I wish you would be serious right now."

"Well then, be straight with me in the asking."

"Okay then, I really want to go to Ireland, but not without you."

"So you think if you make like the trip is about me, I will agree to go." Anna sighed and looked at Jack. A smile broke out, and that smile had always left Jack weak.

Jack stood in silence looking at his wife for the answer. "If Tom says he can spare you from the store, and we can afford to go, then we will go, and may God bless us with a safe trip."

With that said, the trip was on.

CHAPTER VIII

Growing up in poverty, Jack McCarthy had no chance to continue his education by going to college even though he was a great student throughout his years in Salem schools. Anna's family was a bit better off, but it was unusual for girls to attend college in that period. Both had entered the workforce immediately after high school graduation. Making a modest income, they had little money for things other than necessities.

Travelling over to Ireland was something Jack and Anna never dreamed they would be able to do. The very idea of it had the two of them in a constant state of euphoria. It was also the talk of the neighborhood that the young couple would be headed back to the old sod as part of the Sullivan entourage at the height of the prizefighter's fame. Many a lunch hour at the store had featured discussions about Ireland and what was happening there. The entire neighborhood was excited to learn of the details of the trip when the couple returned.

On October 27, 1887, they set sail out of Boston aboard the steamer *Cephalonice*. Anna had traveled to America by steamer as a very young girl, but this was Jack's maiden voyage. The couple looked at it as the wedding trip they had never been able to take. In addition to Jack, Anna, and Sullivan, the group included Jack Ashton, the champ's longtime sparring partner, his trainer, Bill Madden, his female companion, Pat McGowan, and Dan Foley. The champ was the "on-board celebrity" who naturally received a lot of attention from autograph seekers as well as other passengers who just wanted to talk.

On November 6, the ship docked in Liverpool to begin the tour of the British Isles. To Jack and Anna, the opening days in Britain were really of no interest. They would tag along with the champ to various events, but the Ireland leg of the journey was their interest. The itinerary in Ireland included a stop in Kilkenny, Anna's place of birth. For her, this was the highlight of the trip. She would have an opportunity to see aunts, uncles, and cousins she had never met. To Jack, he was anxious to meet with leaders of the Irish Republican Brotherhood and to meet in Cork with his relatives on his mother's side. He would also have the opportunity through meeting these relatives to find out much more about what became of his father's family. Similarly, Pat McGowan was looking forward to getting to Ireland, but he did have a meeting of importance scheduled in Britain.

For the first few weeks following their arrival, the champ was ushered around to various sporting clubs and introduced as the Heavyweight Champion of the World. At the famous Pelican Club in London, he announced to the crowd that it was his fervent desire to fight the English champion, Jem Smith, while he was in Europe, but he didn't think Smith had the same level of enthusiasm. He made it clear that he did not feel Smith dared to get into the ring with him. This type of talk obviously did not sit well with his English audience, but to the Irish, it was great fodder.

While in England, Sullivan also made no attempt to hide his Irish sympathies. He actually accepted an invitation to breakfast at St. James Barracks and dined with the Scots Guards, a regiment well-known for their long and dubious history of combat in Ireland. He met the Prince of Wales, the future King Edward VII, at a fencing club. The Prince presented Sullivan with a matching set of emeralds. When they parted, the champ shook his hand and promised the Prince a high time if he could make it over to Boston. The Prince was extremely impressed with the champ and later described Sullivan as "A marvel of a man. I've never seen anyone like him."

At many of the stops, a sparring exhibition between Sullivan and his sparring partner, Jack Ashton, was part of the entertainment. At these events, Jack would work in the champ's corner. Little actual work was involved as these were just exhibitions, and Ashton was in no shape to seriously box with the champ. Even though they were not serious bouts, the crowds were very enthusiastic and appreciative. Just seeing the champ move around the ring was impressive enough.

After one such event in London, Pat McGowan came over to Jack and told him he had a very important dinner meeting that night with none other than Charles Steward Parnel, and he asked Jack to join him. The invitation was enthusiastically accepted as Jack was not about to pass up an opportunity to meet this great Irish patriot who was the leading spokesman in Parliament for the home rule initiative.

Charles Stewart Parnel was in some ways an unlikely hero of the Irish cause. He was born in Wicklow, Ireland, into an Anglo-Irish Protestant landowning family, a class not normally sympathetic to the idea of Irish Home Rule or Irish independence. He attended English boarding schools and eventually Cambridge, yet he maintained a decidedly anti-British, pro-Irish opinion of the future of Ireland. He was elected to the British House of Commons in 1875 from Meath and quickly became the leading spokesman for Irish Home Rule.

Pat McGowan and Dan Foley, among others in America, had been financially supportive of the push for home rule. They also supported the more radical Irish Republican Brotherhood and saw home rule as merely an interim step to achieving independence. Parnel had not expressed support for this more radical step, and Pat's meeting was to discuss home rule and not delve into more controversial matters.

The meeting was held over dinner and began with introductions. Attending were Pat, Dan Foley, Jack, Parnel, and his aide. Parnel was an impressive figure, tall and strong of stature. Parnel thanked Pat for his support, and Pat complimented Parnel on his work.

Parnel explained that the Home Rule Bill had been introduced by Prime Minister Gladstone, but the vote failed due to a split in Gladstone's liberal party. He explained that going forward, they were working to shore up support within the party so they could introduce a second bill. He felt there was always hope as long as Gladstone was the Prime Minister. But now the conservatives had taken control, and there would be no opportunity to reintroduce the bill until the liberal party was back in power. Even then, passage would depend on holding the liberal members together.

Pat touched on the idea of complete Irish independence, and Parnel did not take a position but stated his opinion that it was not likely to happen in the foreseeable future.

Jack, like Parnel's aide, was an interested listener but said little. The conversation was carried by Pat, Foley, and Parnel. Just the idea of being able to attend such a meeting and watch McGowan and Foley in action with someone as prominent as Parnel was exciting. The conversation during after dinner drinks turned more to small talk around the Sullivan tour and broke up around nine thirty. As they walked back to their hotel, Pat asked "So give me your impressions on Mr. Parnel and our discussion."

"A very impressive man. He carries himself well, is very articulate and dedicated to the cause of home rule. He was noticeably noncommittal to the idea of Ireland's independence. That was a bit discouraging."

"You have to remember where he comes from, Jack. His family, his ancestors, they were not tenant farmers like ours. They were and are landed people. It is to their advantage to keep things in Ireland the way they are. It's impressive enough that he supports home rule given his background."

"I suppose that's true, Pat. In any case, I appreciate the invitation to attend, I'm hoping on this trip to gain a better understanding of the issues of home rule and independence. I know how they are looked at in America, and I want to get a better feel for how the Irish people themselves view the future."

"You will be getting that, Jackie boy, believe me. But not until we cross the water to Ireland." They got back to the hotel, and Jack filled Anna in on the meeting with Parnel.

"It was very impressive to be there to witness the interaction between Pat and a man as impressive as Parnel."

"I'm sure it was Jack, but just think tomorrow, we go to Ireland. I think tonight's meeting will pale by comparison to what we see there."

Parnel continued to push for home rule throughout his political career. Unfortunately, this friend of the Irish had his career cut short by scandal, but the movement pushed on without him.

CHAPTER IX

Ireland

The reception that the group received in Ireland was phenomenal. They arrived on Sunday, December 11, and were met by a huge crowd when they docked at Carlisle Pier in Kingstown. That crowd proved to be small compared to the later crowd that greeted them when they arrived at Westland Row Station. Sullivan gave a speech to a huge adoring Dublin crowd from the drawing room window at the hotel where they were staying. He took great pleasure in reminding them all that he was one of them. Ireland was the birthplace of his parents. He was truly the conquering hero to the Irish people.

He was the guest of honor at a boxing promotion at Leinster Hall. The crowd included the Commander of the British Forces in Ireland, the Prince of Saxe-Weimar. The presence of the commander did not stop Sullivan from mentioning in his speech his sympathy with the Irish struggles for independence, a position that obviously aggravated the commander. Standing in the crowd taking this all in, Jack beamed with pride and heartfelt respect for his friend having the courage to express these views no matter who was in attendance. His admiration for Sullivan grew, and his confidence in his own position on the issue was strengthened by the knowledge that this great champion professed his support openly and proudly.

As in the stops at sporting clubs in England, on Irish stops, Sullivan refereed some amateur bouts and sparred with Jack Ashton. In Waterford, Sullivan was scheduled for yet another sparring session at the Theatre Royal. On the way to Waterford, there was a stopover in Kilkenny where, as usual, they were greeted by a huge crowd.

This being the birthplace of Anna, the crowd included a good few Hennessey first cousins. Anna's father and brother had immigrated to America, but they left behind three sisters and two more brothers who all settled in the Kilkenny area, married, and had children, most of whom Anna had never met. The few that she had met, she did not remember because she was so young. This being the case, Jack and Anna had planned to skip the Waterford stop and spend time in Kilkenny and then rejoin the main group in Cork. To Anna, this was the high point of the entire trip.

They were welcomed to the home and farm of Anna's uncle, Collin, and a group of no less than twenty-seven Hennessey relatives all gathered to have a bit of food and drink at Collin's farm. Meeting ten aunts and uncles and seventeen cousins was overwhelming to Anna. She spent much of the night trying to remember names. Jack was overwhelmed as well in meeting all these relatives of his wife. He was particularly struck by the strong family resemblance. The young Hennessey women were all stunningly beautiful like Anna. The males were full of questions about the champ as well as life in America. The women were less interested in prizefighting and more interested in life in America and questions about the two Hennessey brothers that left and how their families were doing in their new country. Anna was happy to report that her parents and aunt and uncle were prosperous and happy in their new country.

Jack did manage to squeeze in a few questions about the Irish Republican Brotherhood and the push for independence. The older Hennesseys were less enthusiastic on the subject than were the younger family members, but all felt independence was desirable and would happen sooner or later. Anna's cousin, Martin, a feisty seventeen-year-old, showed the most enthusiasm for the cause. He told Jack that he fully planned to join the IRB as he got older. Several of his friends felt the same way. Jack was encouraged by Martin's enthusiasm as well as by the general feeling that independence was inevitable.

The whiskey, food, and conversation rolled on to the wee hours. Some of the more musical members of the group broke out guitars and fiddles and played a good bit of Irish music. A bit of Irish step dancing accompanied the music. It was a grand time, and Jack was welcomed into the fold and treated like part of the family. In the morning, a full Irish breakfast sent them on their way back to the train station to rejoin the group. Hugs and some tears sent them off, and Jack remarked to Anna that he felt he had married into one of Ireland's great families, and she in her sarcastic witty way told him he was lucky they let him in. In spite of the good time and warm reception, Anna was noticeably sad in leaving, but she left with a bucket-load of letters for the family back home.

The couple arrived in Cork on Wednesday, December 14, and rejoined the main group. An article in that morning's paper featured an interview with Sullivan in which he said the main reason he came was to fight the English champ but he had been "blackguarded" out of that fight because Jem Smith was afraid of him. So he had agreed to fight another Englishman, Charlie Mitchel, at a later date instead. He went on to say that he was looking forward to fighting the local amateur Frank Creedon that evening. The local paper described Creedon as "the only man this side of the ocean to stand in against Sullivan."

McGowan had arranged a luncheon meeting at one o'clock at the hotel with Seamus McGary, the treasurer of the Irish Republican Brotherhood. As with the Parnel meeting, Jack accompanied Pat and Dan Foley to the meeting. The IRB was founded by James Stephens in 1858. Stephens was wounded in the "young Ireland" rebellion of 1848 in Ballengary County Tipperary. He was viewed as a hero by the Irish. His associate, John O'Mahoney, founded the US-affiliated organization, the Fenian Brotherhood, to which Jack belonged, around the same time. In 1887, the IRB organization was run by an eleven-person supreme council with three officers: a president, a secretary, and a treasurer. As treasurer, McGary was well aware of Pat McGowan and the financial help that had come from the Boston group. McGary presented himself as a no-nonsense type who was all business, a very serious demeanor honed by years of dealing with Irish resistance.

The meeting began with McGowan explaining that Foley and Jack had taken the oath of the Fenian Brotherhood and McGary could feel comfortable speaking in front of them. McGary proceeded to bring them up-to-date. "We can't be too careful in these matters. British sympathizers are the bane of our organization. We have been very grateful for your financial support from Boston, and we continue to organize for a push to independence. We are convinced that it will only be achieved through armed conflict, and we are a long way from being ready for that eventuality. But it will come."

Pat asked, "What needs to be done in terms of planning, and how can we help?"

"We are in the stages of creating a military council to train Irish volunteers and eventually create a citizens' army. Money is important, but more than that, we need guns to equip our forces. We have been buying guns from Germany, but guns and ammunition from America would be of paramount importance. Right now, we don't have enough equipment for training. Volunteers have to share what little we have to work with."

"I can organize gun and ammunition purchases in America, but getting them here is a problem." Pat was well aware that the British kept an eye out for such shipments.

"We have allies in the shipping business, and if you are the contact person, we will have them work through you to make the arrangements."

This conversation planted the seeds for what would become a weapons connection between Boston and Ireland. As in the Parnel meeting, Jack said little but listened intently. The importance of the conversation was not lost on him, and when they all shook hands at the end of the evening, he knew that he wanted to play a part in future developments. He was impressed with McGary. The confidence with which he spoke of the drive for independence gave Jack confidence it would happen.

"Pat, I want to help in this effort. My business in Salem is doing very well, and I will talk with Tom about contributing to this cause," Jack offered as they walked from the Victoria Hotel.

"We would welcome your participation, Jack, but there is more involved than money. This is an illegal activity, and there may be consequences."

"I know. I'm prepared for that."

"I just want to be sure you know what you are getting into."

Jack nodded his consent, and when they shook hands, they both knew what lay ahead.

They went back to the hotel to get ready for that evening's planned activities. Yet another exhibition of Sullivan's prizefighting ability was planned.

The exhibition was to take place at the Cork Opera House, and the place was packed. Sullivan, ready to fight, took one look at the 5'7" 160-pound Creedon and declared him "not in my class." He complimented the amateur boxer and suggested that instead of fighting him, it would be better if he fought Jack, who was about the same size. Jack resisted the idea, given that his last serious fight was eight years past, but Sullivan and the crowd talked him into it. Thus the exhibition featured Sullivan sparring with Jack Ashton for four rounds, and Jack McCarthy sparring with Frank Creedon for four rounds with Sullivan refereeing.

The bouts were staged using Marquis of Queensbury rules with gloves, and Jack gave a good account of himself. While he obviously was a bit rusty, he managed to land a few good punches and to avoid another broken nose. At the end, Sullivan ruled Creedon had won the bout, and he presented him with a gold medal and again complimented him on his bravery, all of which went over well with the hometown crowd. Jack was feeling that Sullivan's ruling was a bit generous towards his opponent, but he understood it was important to play to the crowd, so he let it go. However, he made sure to mention it to Sullivan when they were alone.

On the morning of December 15, Jack met with Sean Cashman and Grainne Curren, the two siblings of his mother, and Uncle Pat in the restaurant of the Victoria Hotel. Both had been in periodic contact with Johanna and Pat through letters over the years and were well versed on the American families.

At Johanna's request, they had done some research on the famine years in Skibereen and specifically the McCarthy family. As they met with Jack and Anna, they dreaded giving the news of what they had found. It was not a pleasant story. Skibereen was hit hard by the famine, and the McCarthy family of Skibereen had suffered terribly during the famine.

Sean began, "First of all, Jack, you need to know that McCarthy is a great Gaelic name and is an important and revered name in the history of the Skibereen area. They were wealthy overlords with a family castle until they forfeited their estate in the seventeenth century."

"That's interesting history, Sean, but I'm well aware that my grandfather, Mike, was anything but wealthy. I know he sent my father, John, and his brother James to America, although James never made it there. We have never known what happened to the rest of the family."

"I understand, and we have been trying to get as much information as we can, but I have to tell you, it is not a pleasant story."

"I did not expect that it would be, but my brother and I need to know."

Sean nodded his understanding and looked over at his sister for support. With a heavy sigh, he began the story.

Skibereen was one of the earliest and hardest hit areas of Ireland during the famine. As early as 1845, a full one-third of the potato crop was lost to the blight. What's more, the effects of the famine lingered on in Skibereen long after things had begun to improve in other parts of the country. It was the center of some of the most harrowing suffering in the country. The area was so devastated, and bitterness against the lack of a British response was so intense, that it became known as the Cradle of Fenianism. The Irish revolutionary Jeremiah O'Donovan Rossa became politically active in Skibereen right after the famine and is seen as such a hero there that a park had been named in his memory.

Over one-third of the entire population of the area starved to death during the famine. Many others left the area. The McCarthys were not only not spared from this carnage, they were a family particularly hard hit.

"Your grandfather Mike, his wife, and three remaining children were thrown out of their wee cottage in 1849 by their landlord. That we can establish as true. What happened after that is more difficult to verify, but there is no record of any of the five of them in either church or public records after their eviction."

"Could they have moved from the area?" Jack asked.

"It's possible, but very unlikely. We did check public records in the towns in the area and in other parishes. We found no trace of them. After their eviction, there is no record anywhere of their existence."

"The parish priest, Father O'Donovan, has been there for forty years, and he told us with some certainty that he remembers the entire McCarthy family as being among the starving deaths."

This news, while not unexpected, jolted Jack. A dose of reality that he felt would be coming but still shocked and saddened him. It was well-known that over a million Irish starved to death during the famine, but to have it driven home that his ancestors were among those who starved was still a shock.

He asked, "What of Mike McCarthy's siblings?"

"Well, his sister, Pauline, died a spinster in Cork in 1868. According to records at the church, by the time of the famine, your grandfather had already outlived two of his siblings who died very young. After the famine, there is no record of McCarthys in Skibereen or in the immediate area. Again, Father O'Donovan does not recall any of them surviving."

Jack sat silent looking down at the table. Anna reached over and rubbed his back in an attempt to give comfort. Finally looking up, he asked, "Is there a grave for my grandparents that I could visit?"

Sean hesitated to answer and again looked at Grainne before saying, "I'm sorry to say, Jack, that it appears they were all buried in coffinless mass graves along with hundreds of other famine casualties. There is no record in the church, and Father O'Donovan said there was no funeral other than a mass said for the all those who starved to death."

A silence engulfed the table for an extended time until Grainne spoke, "Jack, Anna, I know this has been a terrible conversation, but can you join us tonight for dinner to meet your Irish relatives before you leave tomorrow?"

Anna answered for the two of them as Jack seemed to have been stunned into silence. "We will be happy to be there and appreciate your invitation."

Jack spoke, "I thank you both for taking the time to research all this, I know it's not pleasant news, and it was difficult to relay it all to me. Right now, I would just like to take a walk and do some thinking, but yes, we will be glad to come tonight."

With that, he rose and embraced his aunt and uncle and walked away. Anna spent a few minutes talking with Sean and Grainne to try and break the tension and then followed Jack. She found him a short distance from the hotel sitting on a bench, his head in his hands, crying. She sat next to him, putting her arms around him without saying a word. They sat in silence except for periodic sobs from Jack for over a half hour. Nothing needed to be said.

Later that afternoon, they stood outside the Victoria waiting to be picked up to go to Sean Cashman's house to meet and have dinner with the clan. Jack had said nothing about the morning's discussion all day long. Anna took his hand and, looking at him, asked, "Are you all right, love?"

Jack turned to her and made his first statement. "All that suffering and death, and there was no help from the rich landowners or the British government. No help." He finished in an angry tone.

"I know it hurts, Jack, but it was a long time ago."

"They were my grandparents and my aunts and uncles, and they died a horrible death and then were thrown in a hole with other dead. Not even a Christian burial. I can't get it out of my mind, and I hate the thought of telling Tom and Ma. One thing is for certain. The British grip that has held this country must be broken. The suffering the Irish have endured can all be traced back to them. I will speak no more about it on this trip."

Between them, Sean and Grainne had nine children and nineteen grandchildren. The ages went from the youngest grandchild at two to Sean Jr., age thirty. The entire clan met to greet their American relatives. A number of dishes were brought to the event so there was plenty of food, ranging from shepherd's pie to bacon and cabbage to Irish stew and soda bread. As was the custom, there was plenty of drink as well. Just as in Kilkenny, meeting these many new faces all at once was overwhelming.

Jack made every effort to be cheerful and pleasant to all his newfound relatives, but the overall mood was not as festive as the dinner with the Hennessey family had been, and Jack's somber mood was a big part of that. The subject of the morning discussion was not broached. Instead, there were questions about life in America and what it was like to travel with the champ. Anna had tintypes of Johanna and Tom, which she passed around to all. Several of his cousins had attended the exhibition the night before and complimented Jack on his prizefighting skills. This brought the only laugh Jack could manage all evening. Jack heard a number of stories about Johanna growing up in Killy Donaghue from Sean and Grainne. The stories lifted his spirit and brought him somewhat out of his somber mood. All in all, a pleasant evening, and Jack left with a fistful of letters to be delivered to his mother. In spite of the unpleasant report on the fate of the McCarthys, Jack was glad they had made the stop.

Cork was the last stop on the trip for Jack and Anna. On Friday, December 16, 1887, they sailed out of Cobh Harbor just as their parents had years before and were back in Boston three days after Christmas. The Sullivan group continued onto Limerick then back to Dublin and up to Belfast. The trip, particularly the Ireland portion, proved very lucrative, and the receptions, even in Protestant Belfast, were overwhelming. He went from Belfast to Scotland, where the talk was all about how fellow Irishman Jake Kilrain had fought the English champ Jem Smith to a 106-round draw.

Sullivan never got to fight Smith. He did fight Englishman Charlie Mitchel in France on March 10, 1888. The bare-knuckle fight under London Prize Ring Rules went thirty-nine grueling rounds before being stopped by local authorities. While Sullivan escaped, Mitchel was arrested and brought to jail for the illegal activity. Sullivan got away and headed back to America.

Kilrain, for his part, bragged that his fight with Smith put him on par with Sullivan in terms of any claim to a championship.

Sullivan was annoyed with such talk and would put the matter to rest at his first opportunity. He instructed his handlers to set up a fight with Kilrain "any time, any place, winner takes all." With that, the die was cast for another great bout for the champ.

CHAPTER X

Jack and Anna docked in Boston early on December 29. In spite of being extremely tired, they went straight to the train station and caught the train into Salem. Anna was anxious to tell her family about her visit to Kilkenny and meeting all her relatives. Jack just wanted to get home. Once in Salem, they went straight to McCarthy Brothers Store and arrived just as the lunch crowd was wrapping up. They entered to a standing ovation and hugs from Johanna, Tom, and Mary. Once again, Jack was the returning hero. Newspaper stories about Sullivan's tour had made it back to Salem, including an account of Jack's four-round prizefight in Cork. Jack was a bit embarrassed by all the attention that short match was getting. The locals were full of questions about the tour, about Ireland, and about the general condition and feeling of the Irish people. They answered all the questions that were fired at them. They told the stories of the huge receptions the champ received. They described the lives of their relatives, and they explained the unrest of the Irish, including plans for action that Jack heard in his meeting with Parnel, as well as the meeting with the IRB officer. All the stories and accounts of life in the old country were enthusiastically received by the patrons. Finally, Johanna took the floor and announced that she had good news for the couple's return.

The store grew quiet as the highly respected matriarch drew Tom and Mary over to her side and proudly announced, "Your brother, Tom, and sister-in-law, Mary, are going to be parents, and I'm going to be a grandmother."

The locals in the store, many of whom were hearing this for the first time, gave out applause. Jack and Anna congratulated the happy couple and the grandmother-to-be. It all made for a very happy homecoming. They both were happy to be home among family and friends and were very happy for Tom and Mary.

That night, Anna went over to see the Hennessey clan and bring them all up-to-date on her visit to Kilkenny. She handed out all the letters from their relatives while enthusiastically describing her visit. She wanted to leave Jack with his brother and mother to tell them what he had learned of the fate of the McCarthys. The gathering at Mike Hennessey's house was a festive one with stories of his and Bill's siblings and many nieces and nephews. Anna described the farm and all the cousins, aunts, and uncles she had met. Stories of the evening in Kilkenny brought up stories from the brothers about the siblings Anna had met and the times they had growing up together. The stories brought laughter and warm feelings to all in attendance. Anna did tell all in the Hennessey family that Jack was relaying a sadder tale to the McCarthys.

Across Derby Street at the McCarthy home on Becket Street, the mood was far more somber. Jack told the story of Skibereen's devastation and specifically what he had learned of the fate of the McCarthys, right down to the mass graves in which they were buried. When he had finished, the room was silent as the three listeners tried to digest the horrific details. As Anna had done in Ireland, Mary put her arm around Tom to give some comfort.

Johanna broke the silence. "I never wanted to ask for the research to be done because I expected this outcome. I didn't want you boys to know."

"We have to know, Ma. Tom and I have a right to know what the bastard landowners and British government that rule the land did, how they turned their back on the suffering and death."

"I never met any of your father's family. We met on the boat coming over. Your father told me stories of his family, but I never met any of them. Your father never knew what happened to them. I'm glad he never knew. He suffered enough indignity here in America. To add to it with these details of his family would have been cruel. I've never told you boys how bad it was when we arrived. The Boston Brahmins who ran the city all thought they farted with a PH. They had no use for the lowly Irish. Your father and I waited years to get married, hoping he could find steady work to support ourselves and the family we wanted. It was very difficult for Irish immigrants in the fifties."

* * * * *

Boston, Massachusetts, 1849

While the famine had made life in Ireland a desperate struggle, immigrating to America was not a joyful event. In the 1840s, the Irish comprised nearly one half of the immigrants coming to America. In Ireland, when a family member left, it was called an "American Wake" because all knew that they would never again see their departing family member. When they arrived in America, they were met with a new battle for survival. They found they were not welcome in America. No group was considered lower than the Irish, who were held in a position of shame and poverty. Those who could read saw their race ridiculed in the American press with lines in major newspapers like the following:

Scratch a convict or pauper and the chances are that you are tickling the skin of an Irish Catholic

Putting them on a boat and sending them back home would solve the crime in America

Harpers Weekly carried a cartoon depicting a drunken Irishman with the caption "the usual Irish way of doing things."

Johanna Cashman and John McCarthy arrived in Boston in 1849 to be greeted by the strong anti-Irish sentiment that they had not expected. Boats arriving with Irish immigrants were pounced on by "runners," fellow Irish hired by local landlords to offer housing as a way to bilk the arrivals out of their money. John and Johanna were ignored by them because they had so little money. As they looked for lodging, they were greeted by signs in windows announcing no

Irish were welcome. Cities like Boston developed "Irish towns," where Irish banded together, living in basements and shanties. Only a Catholic church shelter was available for the first several nights for the two. Irish were not welcomed as employees either. Many newspaper help wanted advertisements announced "no Irish need apply." Irish like Johanna who could read and write were treated a bit better than those like John who could not. These illiterate immigrants were reduced to begging in the street, which was how John started.

John's venture into a livery stable that he had heard was looking for help was one of his many insults. When he approached the owner with his Irish accent, the man took him by the arm and led him outside, followed by the twelve-person workforce. Pointing to a sign, he asked, "Can you read that?" John shook his head and the man said, "Of course, you can't, you thick fucking mick, none of you can read. It says no dogs, pigs, or Irish. Now get the fuck out of here." He walked away followed by gales of laughter from the assembled employees.

Johanna was more fortunate. Because she could read, the priest at the shelter told her that he had heard from the priest in Salem that there was an opportunity for work as a nanny in that town. Johanna headed north then and in fact was hired as a nanny, separating her from John and her brother.

John's troubles continued in Boston as he could not find steady employment or a place to live. Pat Cashman, like his sister, was able to read and write, so he fared better. He actually found employment with a construction company. He had done carpentry work in Ireland and had a great talent for the trade. He was able to find work because of his skill. John had been a farm laborer in Ireland and was unskilled as well as illiterate. Pat had rented housing and let John sleep in the basement at his place. After a couple of weeks with him not being able to find work, Pat took him to his construction site to see if the foreman would hire John.

The foreman looked at the two of them and said through clenched cigar-chomping teeth, "You're lucky we gave you a job, so don't push it. One dumbass Irishman is enough to deal with for anyone. The only reason we keep you on is to do the jobs nobody else will do."

With the assistance of the same priest who helped Johanna, he found part-time work in Salem dunging out the stables at the municipal fire and police stations. Shoveling horse manure was the best employment he could find, but it did provide a steady, if meager, income. Enough so that he was able to rent a room in "Irish Town." What he called home was an eight-by-ten third-floor room in a boarding house on Derby Street.

Again with the help of the parish priest, Johanna was able to rent the wee ramshackle cottage at 6 Blaney Street. Every morning, rain or shine, snow, ice, or whatever the conditions, she walked the two miles to the home at 38 Chestnut Street to her job as nanny for three children. Chestnut Street was the wealthiest section of Salem populated by merchants and sea captains.

Meanwhile, John tried to improve his employment position and make a steady enough income that they could marry. Johanna would read the help wanted pages to try and find him good employment, but many advertisements would state that "no Irish need apply." On several occasions when that was not stated in the advertisement, when John showed up to apply, he would be told that no Irishman would be hired.

He did gain enough confidence over time at the municipal stables that they began giving him more hours doing repairs to some of the equipment. Eventually, they felt things were stable enough to marry, and they did so at the Immaculate Conception Church. They did so knowing full well that they were consigned to a life of hard work and poverty but in hopes they could do better for their children. Like the rest of the Irish immigrants, they fought back. They fought the anti-Irish sentiment, they ignored the insults, and eventually, the Irish became accepted as Americans. One paper wrote in 1870 that the Irish had become "more Americanized than Americans."

John died when a cart rolled over on him and crushed him when Johanna was pregnant with their second son. He never saw his two sons grow up to have the success he hoped for them. He suffered the indignity of being seen as a dumb useless Irishman right up until the day he died. His death resulted in no mention at all in the local paper and a funeral at the church attended by his wife, brother, and sisters-in-law, and four fellow workers for the city of Salem.

All this history about their poor father had the effect of further depressing the two brothers. It also made them more determined to live the successful life their father envisioned for them. They would work as hard and as long as it took to make that happen.

CHAPTER XI

As the decade of the 1880s was drawing to a close, a number of major events happened in the lives of the McCarthys. Perhaps the most important event was Anna announcing in January 1888 that she was joining her sister-in-law, Mary, and expecting a child. Jack would tell the Derby Street store crowd that while the child would not be born in Ireland, he was conceived in Ireland. In July, Tom and Mary welcomed their first child, a daughter named Margaret. Two months later on September 5, Jack and Anna's first child, a boy, came into the world. Not surprisingly, he was named John L. McCarthy.

Earlier that year, Jack, Tom, and Uncle Pat had attended a ceremony in Boston in which the city presented John L. Sullivan with what became his official heavyweight champion of the world belt. Sullivan had returned from Europe and his bout with Charlie Mitchell in March of 1888. The city presented him with a diamond-encrusted gold belt upon his return. The inscription read "Presented to John L. Sullivan, the Heavyweight Champion of the World." It included a gold harp surrounded by shamrocks to honor his Irish heritage and American flags to honor his home country.

As one would expect, the ceremony was followed by a celebration in a local pub where Sullivan announced he was negotiating a deal to fight with Jake Kilrain and "settle his hash." Kilrain, a fellow Irishman, was also born in Massachusetts, like Sullivan. He was the pride of Summerville, Massachusetts. He had made statements after defeating the English champ that he had as much claim to the championship title as Sullivan. Sullivan wanted to put that to rest. He told Jack he would be starting his training in Boston and hoped Jack would work with him. Jack's time was rapidly becoming less and less his own, and he promised the champ he would do what he could.

Anna had quit her job when they took the trip to Ireland, so on her return, she was helping at the store. Upon the birth of the two grandchildren, both she and Mary were splitting time between minding both children and working at the store. The two mothers also shared time with Anna's sister Bridget, who spent as much time with the children as she could. Johanna also took her turn at taking care of the newborns and was often called on for advice and assistance from the two new mothers. The close proximity of the store and the living quarters made the shared workloads easy to manage.

It had taken both couples some time to have their firstborns, but the second pregnancies came quickly. Jack and Anna were first this time in announcing in January 1889 that Anna was expecting. Six weeks later, Tom and Mary made the same announcement. The McCarthy family seemed to be expanding rather rapidly, and Johanna could not be happier. The grandchildren she always wanted were coming fast.

With all this going on, Jack found precious little time to get to Boston either to assist in the training of the champ or to attend meetings of the Fenian Brotherhood. While he was in Ireland, Peter Grady had quit his job at the cigar manufacturer Battis and Brown in Salem, where he had worked with Jack, and he moved to Boston. He was tending bar three or four nights a week at Southies, and he had become an officer in the Brotherhood. Meetings in Boston had become the only times Jack saw his old friend. He had filled Peter in on what he had learned of the fate of the McCarthys, and it only served to stoke the already intense flames of Peter's feelings toward the British. Jack's loyalty and passion for the cause of the brotherhood, while strong, could not match the passion of his friend Peter.

In spite of Jack not providing any assistance in the training, Sullivan went into his fight with fellow Irishman Jake Kilrain in tremendous shape. It was a heavily gambled and much anticipated fight. They met on July 8, 1889, in Fitchburg, Mississippi, in front of over three thousand spectators. The bout drew worldwide coverage and was staged using London Prize Ring Rules, and it was a bareknuckle brawl. This type of fighting was still not legal and would have consequences for both combatants. It lasted two and a quarter hours and seventy-two rounds until the doctor in attendance and Kilrain's trainer refused to let him get onto the scratch to start another round. The physician had told Kilrain's corner that another round would endanger the game fighter's life.

Sullivan won the fight but then had to face charges from the State of Mississippi for violating the laws against bareknuckle prizefighting. He ended up spending more for attorneys defending himself than he won for the fight. He vowed it would be his last bareknuckle fight, and it was, in fact, not only his last one, but the last heavyweight championship bout fought with bare knuckles. Following this defense of his crown, Sullivan became somewhat inactive. It was unusual for him as he had defended his title in a very active fashion until then. In 1892, an out-of-shape and aging Sullivan would finally lose the title to Jim Corbot. The loss would not affect his friendship with Jack. Although they were seeing less of each other, they remained friends right up until Sullivan's death in 1918.

Back home in Salem, Anna's pregnancy was having its issues. She had gone into false labor several times, and cramping and discomfort were constant. The baby girl came two months early in July and only lived four days. Anna was crushed, and Jack and Johanna did their best to console her. Just like their first child, the baby was born at home and delivered by a midwife with late help from Doctor Philips, who arrived just in time to see the delivery. Jack blamed himself for not making more of an effort to provide the best medical assistance. Home births were the norm in the Irish neighborhood at the time. Jack and his brother were both born at home. Still Jack felt responsible somehow for the baby's death.

"Jack, you can't blame yourself, you did nothing wrong," Johanna told him. "The child came early, there was nothing they could do."

"There must be something I could have done different, Ma. I'm not sure Anna will ever recover."

"She will, Jack. The doctor said there is no reason you can't have more children. That will help her recover."

Anna stayed in bed for several days trying to regain her strength. The postpartum depression was severe, and her normally cheerful happy-go-lucky attitude was nowhere to be found. Jack couldn't even get one of her sarcastic comebacks even after he set her up.

Jack spent every minute he could with her, but he found it difficult to stop her from crying. "We can try again, Anna. Maybe this one was just not meant to be." While she knew there may be more opportunities, it did not console her.

Anna was very religious, but she found herself blaming God. "Why would God do this to us, Jack? We have been good faithful people, and yet we are left to suffer this tragedy." In the depths of her depression, she would make these kinds of statements. Jack would respond trying to bring out her fighting spirit.

"Anna, there are so many in the world who suffer worse tragedies. This will make us stronger. There is a reason for everything even if we don't understand what the reason is."

They looked at each other; Anna shook her head and started to cry again. Jack embraced her as she cried, knowing that only time would heal this wound.

After a week of recovery, she went back to her normal routine of working at the store and taking care of the two youngsters. Still, her depression was apparent. Margaret turned a year old while Anna was recovering, and John L. had his first birthday in September. That event seemed to bring Anna a bit out of her depression. In November, Mary gave birth to Molly, and while the entire family celebrated the healthy birth of the second daughter of Tom and Mary, Anna could not help feeling her depression return. She could not help thinking that her daughter would have grown up as Molly's close cousin and playmate. What finally brought her around was the announcement in December that she was pregnant again.

"We need to pray, Jack, every day, that this is a healthy pregnancy. I will take better care of myself to make sure everything goes right, but we need to pray together every night and every morning."

Jack agreed with the prayer rituals as well as attending mass three times a week with Johanna, who offered up her nightly rosary for the health of this baby. Anna worked fewer hours at the store during this pregnancy and took no chances with her body. The nine months went by without the discomfort of the previous pregnancy, and on July 8, 1890, William McCarthy came into the world a healthy eight-pound boy. It was the salvation of Anna's spirit. She would never forget the baby girl she lost, but she cherished the two healthy sons God gave her and Jack.

The McCarthys moved into the decade of the nineties with four new additions and Mary now pregnant with a fifth. The store had developed into the number one political hot spot in Ward I, the Irish section of the city. Politics on both sides of the Atlantic would be the order of the day throughout the nineties for the family on Derby Street, as Jack would become more and more involved locally, as well as with the American efforts to assist their brothers and sisters in Ireland. He and Anna became a common sight walking the two young boys up and down Derby Street on nights after the store closed, greeting their neighbors all along the way, sharing conversation with everyone they came across. The popularity of the store, their activities in the church, and their constant interaction with their neighbors all served to make Jack and Anna the most popular couple in the neighborhood. There was nobody in the neighborhood more revered than Johanna McCarthy, and no family held in higher regard than the McCarthys.

CHAPTER XII

The first half of the decade of the nineties saw Jack getting more involved in political issues on both sides of the Atlantic. The Second Home Rule Bill was introduced in 1893, and it passed the House of Commons but was defeated in the House of Lords. This was a major setback for the home rule movement. With this defeat, sentiment in Ireland began shifting from home rule to complete independence. Jack was attending meetings of the Fenian Brotherhood as often as he could get away. His Uncle Pat was attending on a regular basis, and of course, Peter Grady was an officer in the organization and extremely active. The defeat of home rule got the same reaction on the American side of the Atlantic. The majority of members of the Brotherhood began to see home rule as a lost cause and independence as the appropriate goal.

The first shipment of guns from the Boston chapter was arranged in the spring of 1892. Jack and his uncle had both contributed money to the cause. Pat McGowan was the largest contributor. A passenger ship, the *Royal Maiden*, which sailed under the Union Jack and carried shipments as well as passengers and captained by a less-than-scrupulous Jack Taggot, would carry six cases of rifles holding twenty rifles apiece, along with ammunition, over the Atlantic.

At a meeting of the Fenian Brotherhood, Pat McGowan explained the arrangements. "It cost us as much to bribe that bastard Taggot as it did to buy the guns. The *Maiden* will be docking at Liverpool, and the cases will be unloaded there and placed on a vessel the IRB will arrange to have there. They will then be brought over to Ireland."

Members were enthusiastic about the prospect of playing this major role in the movement.

"Can we trust Taggot and his crew?" Mike Foley asked.

"Only Taggot and one crew member know what's in the crates, and they would not be able to identify where they came from. We have booked passage on the ship for Peter Grady, who will keep an eye on things. Taggot does not know there is any connection between Grady and the guns. When they reach Liverpool, the IRB people will be looking for passenger Grady, and he will go along to Ireland with the guns."

Peter chimed in, "I'm excited to be a part of this, not only because of the importance of the mission, but also because it will be my first visit to Ireland."

After additional discussion among the group, Jack took his friend Peter aside for a private talk.

"This all sounds pretty dangerous, Pete. Are you sure you know what you are getting into?"

"I'm just an innocent passenger. Nobody on board will know of my connection until I join with the IRB boys. Don't worry, Jackie, I have it all figured out."

Peter's enthusiasm for the cause was not new, but the role he was taking on worried his longtime friend. They had been best friends since their early school days. They later worked together at Battis and Brown. It was one thing to offer financial support to the mission as Jack was doing, quite another to actually participate physically.

"As soon as you get back to the states, come to Salem and let me know you are safe. I will remain concerned until I see you back here."

"Not to worry, Jack. I have it all under control. I will be filling you in on all the details over drinks at O'Shea's before you know it."

The ship sailed on March 20, and as he promised, Peter's safety was on Jack's mind continually from that day forward. Meanwhile, local political issues were also taking up more of his attention. The store was the political hot spot for Ward I, and Jack was being promoted by many of his regulars as the ideal Ward I candidate for elected office. He was obviously interested in the issues of the day and felt he had something to contribute. However, as always, his family and business obligations would have to be addressed. The store was still run by Jack, Tom, Johanna, Anna, and Mary, with the latter two also sharing time taking care of the four children, Margaret, Molly, John, and Bill. In addition, Mary was now pregnant with child number 3. Before making a decision to run for office, Jack knew he would have to discuss it with his family. Without their support, he could not even consider the idea.

He first went to the person who always provided his best advice, Johanna. Johanna's advice was for Jack to talk with Tom and Anna and work things out with them. "You know your obligations, first is to your family. The second is to your business. That's how I raised you."

As always, Tom was the loyal brother always supportive of Jack. "Look, if you run and win, it can only be good for business. Take care of the issues important to Ward I and the people who you represent, and it will work out fine. The meetings are mostly in the evening when we are closed. So if it's all right with Anna, it's all right with me."

For her part, Anna was supportive in her own sarcastic way.

"The talk in the store is all about me running for Common Council, and I would be lying if I said I was not interested. What do you think I should do?"

"If you're asking if we can spare you around here, you are really quite useless anyway, Jack. Tom and Johanna do all the work. I suppose it would be your chance to be the big wheel you've always thought you were." A typical response from her, mixing her sarcastic humor with her advice. It was not what Jack wanted.

"Can you please be serious? I'm trying to make a decision here, and I need your input."

Anna put on a serious face before she responded.

"Okay, seriously, if Tom feels it will work out in terms of the store, I can support the move. I think you would be an excellent representative of the people in Ward I, and they need someone like you carrying the banner. I love you, Jack, and I will support whatever you do, and I don't mind sharing you with the people that need you representing them."

"Anna McCarthy, I love you more every day because every day you give me more insight into the woman you are." They embraced and held each other for a long time, and with that, the die was cast.

In Salem at that time, like most Massachusetts cities, the government was made up of two branches of government: the Common Council and the board of Alderman. The Common Council was elected on a ward-by-ward basis and was typically made up of various ethnic groups, as each ethnic neighborhood would elect one of their own. The Board of Alderman was the more prestigious body and required an election at large on a city-wide basis. It was decided that in the next election, Jack would run for the Common Council representing Ward I. So for the next several months, his work in the store involved campaigning as well as working. His customer base could not have been more supportive. He was an intelligent, articulate person who understood the people he was running to represent. His popularity was well-earned. All encouraged him to run and win. He was confident of the neighborhood support.

Peter Grady returned from Ireland safely and reported that the mission had been a success. The guns were delivered, and he had met the three governing officers of the IRB. He returned home more excited about and committed to the cause than ever. He kept his promise reporting directly to Jack in Salem.

"Jack, I tell you, it was the biggest thrill of my life. I spent some time with the very people who are planning an uprising. They are terrific, and believe me, they are working night and day to achieve their goal." It was Peter's first trip to Ireland, and while Jack was interested in the details of his meetings, he was just as interested in his impression of the country.

"Isn't the country beautiful, Pete?"

Peter went into a discussion of his travels around the country. The natural beauty of it made him even more outraged that so many Irish had to leave, especially his own family.

"Oh, if scenery were money, all the Irish would be rich. But the poverty is awful, widespread, and awful. The British see Ireland only as a source of resources that will make their lives comfortable. They care nothing for the people. We need to break the hold the English arseholes have on the country that beats down our people."

"Your commitment to that end is incredible. Speaking of incredible, I'm running for the Common Council."

Peter fell back in mock horror at the suggestion. "You would be a great representative of this neighborhood. How will you ever find the time?"

"That is the question. First I have to get elected, then we will find out."

"Who is going to beat you in this neighborhood? Everybody likes you and the whole McCarthy clan."

"Well, right now there is nobody running against me, but time will tell I guess."

Peter hung around until the store closed, and then he and Jack went upstairs to the apartment and had dinner with Anna and the kids. Anna greeted him with a warm embrace. "Peter, I'm so happy to see you. It's been forever. You look no worse for wear, I guess."

"That's the nicest thing you ever said to me."

With that, he and Jack played with the two kids while Anna fixed dinner. It was a great evening that reminded all of them of the days when Peter was still in Salem and they were all younger.

The three friends talked and laughed through dinner and then were joined by Tom. The camaraderie went on to the wee hours, and Peter spent the night on the couch in the apartment and headed back to Boston the next morning.

In the Common Council election in 1893, Jack won easily over a less-than-enthusiastic opponent named Connor Griffin. In winning, he received 74 percent of the vote, a truly impressive total for the first-time candidate. He established himself early on as an active and outspoken member of the council who fought hard for issues important to Ward I. Tom's prediction about it being good for the store also proved out. Jack's importance on the council enhanced the trade in the store, as it seemed everyone in the ward wanted a piece of his time, and the best place to get him was at the store.

On the downside, it meant even less free time for him. Between the store, the two young boys, and the council, he had little time for anything else including meetings of Fenian Brotherhood.

The second shipment of guns was being planned for 1894. As before, they would use the *Royal Maiden* and bribe Captain Taggot. Peter Grady had once again volunteered for the escort job, but there was a feeling that two trips over in two years would be seen as a bit suspicious. Peter made the case that he was still the perfect choice because he knew the operation and how it was supposed to go. In the end, it was agreed that Peter would go, but under the assumed name of John O'Brian. The ship was set to sail at the end of March out of Boston Harbor. As before, Jack made him promise to report to Salem as soon as he was back safely. The night before the ship left, Peter spent the night with Jack and Anna. They were joined again by Tom and shared dinner and good conversation well into the evening reminiscing about old times. None of them knew it at the time, but it would be the last evening they would ever share together. Peter shipped out the following morning.

Jack and Anna's two boys were growing fast. John L., who was called by everyone Jack Junior, was looking to his sixth birthday in September. Bill would be four in July. They were both fixtures in the store, and Jack Junior would be starting in the Salem School system in the fall. Johanna was already working with him at home, teaching him how to read, as well as basic arithmetic. Anna's sister, Bridget, also spent a good deal of time with both boys reading to them and playing games. The proximity of the families, the Hennesseys across Derby Street and Uncle Tom and grandmother Johanna right behind the store, gave the boys a real sense of security and solid family support. Their cousins, Margaret and Molly, were roughly the same age and joined in the various games Bridget, Jack, and Tom would organize. Tom and Mary's third child was a boy. Tom named him John after his father, so now there were five youngsters to deal with. There were constant games being organized and played around the store and the Hennessey home.

Jack's political career was also blossoming as he had distinguished himself very early and caught the attention of a real rising political star in John Hurley. Altogether, life was moving along very well for the McCarthys. The first hint of trouble in their world came when Uncle Pat came in the store one Saturday afternoon and pulled Jack aside for a conversation. As they walked out of the store, they headed up Derby Street for a private conversation.

"Bad news from across the pond, I'm afraid. McGowan received a cable saying the IRB crew that was in Liverpool to receive the guns have all been arrested by British officials."

This news stopped Jack in his tracks. He looked at his uncle and asked, "My god, Pat, what went wrong and what of Peter Grady?"

"I'm afraid Peter was also detained. The rifles were confiscated, as was the boat the IRB sent over. McGowan is trying to get the details on what went wrong. The whole operation was a disaster."

Jack was absolutely stunned by the news. "What will they do with them all? Do we have any idea?"

"Details will be coming, but I really don't know any more right now than I've told you. There's a meeting of the Fenian Brotherhood tonight. If you can make it, Jack, it will be important."

"I will do my best to make it, Pat. This is awful. I feel sick to my stomach."

The two went back to the store. Pat visited with his sister while Jack went back to work. He filled Tom in on what happened, making it difficult for both brothers. They were both worried sick.

That night, Jack went into Boston with his uncle to attend the meeting. Pat McGowan had received two more cables that explained more details. Irish Republican Brotherhood officials believed that Captain Taggot had not only taken a bribe to ship the guns, he had taken another one from the British to turn in the parties involved. In short, he had double-crossed the Brotherhood. The four IRB members who met the ship have been charged with treason. Peter Grady was being held for questioning. The British were interested in getting all the information they could about US organizations that were involved in aiding the IRB. Taggot had told them what he knew, but they had been careful not to let him know too much about where the money and guns came from. The British felt that they could learn a lot more from Peter Grady. Depending on what more they learned and how much US officials would cooperate with their investigation, members of the Fenian Brotherhood could be questioned or even charged. This was of course troubling news for everyone. The idea that they may well be in trouble as a group was disturbing. More disturbing was the fact that their friend, Peter Grady, was in British custody.

Discussion after this briefing was subdued as members were obviously worried. The general consensus was that Peter would not give out any information, but everyone there knew that he would be tortured. Given that it was impossible to feel 100 percent sure he would not give in to the interrogation, the group broke up with everyone walking away concerned with their future.

Jack, Pat McGowan, Mike Foley, and Pat Cashman went out for a drink and discussed things further. "This could be the end of our whole organization," McGowan opined. "God knows what they will do with Peter."

Mike Foley chimed in, "We are absolutely going to have to lie low for a while even if we do stay together as an organization."

Four very serious looking faces brooded over their drinks while they contemplated what else might happen. Jack spent the night at his uncle's. It was a somber evening.

Jack went back to Salem expecting anytime for another shoe to drop. He told Tom about the whole thing but said nothing to Anna or his mother, thinking it better to wait for more details. Two weeks went by with no word reaching Salem about any further investigation or any resolution to Peter Grady's situation. Jack went about his work, but the thought of his good friend's situation never left his mind.

On May 10, Pat McGowan and Pat Cashman came in the store and asked Jack to take a walk with them. As they walked down Derby Street, Jack knew the news would not be good.

His uncle opened the conversation. "Look, this is not easy for me to tell you this, but brace yourself, Jack. We got news yesterday that Peter Grady hanged himself in his cell two days ago."

It was like getting hit with a bolt of lightning. His knees actually buckled. "Oh, god, no, no. He would never do that, never!"

His uncle grabbed him for support or he may well have fallen to the ground.

"We have no idea what they have been putting him through. They probably drove him to it," said McGowan.

"No, I know Peter better than anyone in this world. He would not do this. They killed him. They killed him and made it look like a suicide. Those bastards!" He was absolutely convinced that Peter would never kill himself no matter what they did to him.

They walked a bit further until Jack said he would appreciate it if they would let him be alone. His uncle asked if he was sure he was all right, and Jack said he was, but he wanted to be alone. McGowan said something about further British investigation. Jack replied that he no longer cared and walked off by himself. They watched him walk away with his shoulders slouched. They both felt they had never seen a sadder looking man.

He walked along Salem Harbor for a long time, getting back to the store almost two hours later. His uncle and McGowan had already left for Boston. Jack told Tom the sad news and went upstairs to tell Anna. She took the news as badly as Jack, and the two of them stood in each other's arms and cried for what seemed hours, both feeling it was the saddest day of their lives. Peter Grady had been Jack's best friend all his life. The thought of him dying at the hands of the British was more than Jack could stand.

In London, a very inebriated Captain Jack Tagget stumbled out of a pub to head home. He did not notice the three rough looking Irishmen that followed him as he left. Three weeks later, news reached the Boston Fenians that the dead mutilated body of a Captain Taggot was found in a London alley. It had been confirmed that he betrayed the IRB. Obviously, they made him pay for that betrayal. The news provided little consolation to the friends of Peter Grady.

CHAPTER XIII

The Boston police chief, Dave Evans, was a huge, rugged man. At six foot, three inches, and 225 pounds, he was an imposing figure. He worked his way up from patrolman, and the time behind a desk had not softened him up at all.

On the morning of January 18, 1895, the chief sat in his office awaiting a visit from federal officials, a Mr. Archibald from the State Department, Steven Johnson, the local US Marshal, and two British officials named Myers and Davis. He knew and had dealt with Johnson, whom he considered to be as useless as tits on a bull, just another do-nothing federal paycheck. The other three were strangers. He had no idea what they wanted, and he was not looking forward to their arrival.

Evans rose to meet the four of them as they entered his office. They all shook hands as introductions were made, and then they all sat around the conference table in his office. After a bit of small talk, Archibald got into the reason for the meeting.

"Chief Evans, there have been some disturbing events in the United Kingdom and in our own country that involve organizations here in Boston as well as New York and other US cities. The British government has asked for our help in addressing the actions of these organizations. I will let these gentlemen explain in more detail."

With that, he turned things over to the two men from Britain. Myers took the lead. "Thank you, Mr. Archibald. Chief Evans, Mr. Davis and I are part of a special task force in the embassy of the United Kingdom. Our job is to monitor and, to the extent possible, interfere with the plans of the Fenian Brotherhood here in the United States. This is a group made of misguided Irish Americans who are supporting a treasonous movement in the United Kingdom. We have been aware for some time that guns were being shipped from Boston, as well as New York, to Ireland in a misguided effort to support the Irish Republican Brotherhood. That group in Ireland is intent on initiating an armed insurrection to achieve Irish independence. The gun shipments are obviously illegal. The entire movement is considered treason by her majesty's government."

Davis picked it up from there. "Several months ago, a shipment of guns from Boston was seized by authorities on the Liverpool docks. We detained a man from Boston, one Peter Grady, and began questioning him about the Boston organization. Mr. Grady was a rather rough sort, so we were unable to gain any information from him. Unfortunately, he hanged himself in his cell, ending the opportunity. However, we did gain some information from the ship's captain, a Mr. Taggot. In spite of the efforts on this end to keep him in the dark, Taggot learned of an organization here in Boston that initiated the shipment, a chapter of the Fenian Brotherhood. The only name he was aware of was a Patrick McGowan."

Chief Evans had sat silently listening up to this point but spoke up here. "Patrick McGowan is an important leading citizen in this community, a real leader with a strong financial base."

"We have done our research on him," Myers said. "We know that is true. Still we intend to talk with him."

Evans knew McGowan very well. His thought was *good luck trying to gain any information from him*. He kept that thought to himself and said, "So what do you want from my department?"

"We would like the cooperation of the department in identifying the members of the organization so we can question them to find out the extent of their activities in Ireland."

Evans looked at Archibald and asked, "What's the state department's role here?"

"We always cooperate with our allies. We agreed to set up this meeting and to offer the services of the US Marshal's offices."

Evans looked at Johnson, who simply nodded his agreement. Evans knew from past experience that the nod would be the most effort Johnson would put into the matter. Evans did not want to be in the middle of any effort to question, or in any way lean on Pat McGowan. What's more, he knew full well that the general population in Boston would not look favorably on his department working with the British.

"With all due consideration to the United Kingdom, this does not strike me as a matter for the Boston Police Department."

Myers responded, "I understand that, Chief, but all we are asking is any information your men would have about the membership of this organization."

The chief nodded at this and figured the best way to end this was to cooperate.

"Well, I will speak to my sergeants to alert them to the effort. We will find out what the members of the force know about any of this. To whom would we share whatever we are able to find?"

Evans was given the contact information for the two men from Britain. With that the meeting adjourned. They all shook hands as the four visitors left. Evans sat back down at his desk, chuckling to himself. Half of his force was Irish. His most trusted lieutenant was Seamus O'Mally. The degree of cooperation he would expect from the troops was not very high. Still he sent word out that he wanted to see O'Mally.

The meeting with Lieutenant O'Mally took place at two o'clock that afternoon. O'Mally was only slightly smaller that Evans, a rough, tough Boston Irishman with red hair and the map of Ireland on his face. The two officers went back a good number of years on the Boston police force. They worked together on many occasions, sharing a very good relationship of mutual respect.

Evans opened the meeting explaining about his visit earlier that day. He finished by relaying the request that members of the force help identify the members of the organization.

O'Mally responded, "Do you really want to get involved in this, Chief?"

"What do you mean?"

"This city is full of Irish sympathizers. Pat McGowan is the most popular Irishman in Boston with the lone exception of John L. himself."

"Do you know of this organization?"

"I'm certainly aware, Chief, that there are a lot of Irish in Boston who have strong feelings about what is happening in Ireland. I also know they have no love for the British. I don't think our cooperation on a British initiative is going to be good for public relations or for the morale of our own men."

Evans stood up and walked to the window, looking out with his hands clasped behind his back. He knew O'Mally was right. He suspected his lieutenant was more than aware of the organization in question. He suspected O'Mally was probably a member. He further suspected that the membership probably included a few more of his officers. He reflected on this for a time as O'Mally sat in silence.

Finally he turned back to O'Mally. "This is what we are going to do. You wait a few days then go see that nitwit Marshal Johnson. Tell him you have spoken with your men to see if there was any knowledge of this pro-Irish group and you came up empty. Tell him our men are sniffing around and if anything turns up, we will get the information to him."

"I can do that all right, Chief, but how will you handle the two Brits?"

"I will deal with them. I plan to get word to them that I feel it will be better if the department deals directly with Johnson. It will be better for our community relations to not deal directly with a foreign government. When nothing turns up, we will shift the blame on to that dumbass Johnson."

"Sounds like a plan, Chief." With that, O'Mally got up and walked out of the office.

Chief Evans sat back down at his desk giving his plan of action a bit more thought. After a few moments, he shrugged his shoulders, chuckled to himself again, and moved on to something else. He never gave it another thought. The British officials never heard anymore from the Boston police force.

As soon as his shift ended, Seamus O'Mally left police headquarters and went straight to Pat McGowan's office. Upon arriving there, he interrupted a meeting Pat was in with a number of his employees. He signaled Pat to join him in a private conversation.

"The chief had a visit today from a couple of Brits and a state department flunky. They were looking for help in identifying the members of the Brotherhood."

"Were you in the meeting?"

"No, Chief brought me in later."

"Does Chief Evans know you're in the Brotherhood?"

"No, he doesn't. I wanted you to know that he's not going to take any action to help them. The only name they have right now is you. So I expect you will be getting a visit."

McGowan just smiled at this news. He was not concerned about the visit. He thanked his good friend for the heads up and assured him that he would handle any visit from the two Brits.

CHAPTER XIV

The second half of the decade of the nineties started off positive as Jack ran for alderman as part of the John F. Hurley ticket. He won the election, and Hurley's "big four" included Jack, and this group would run Salem city government for the next twelve years. During those years, Jack would serve in a number of capacities, including foreman of the street department and assistant tax assessor. His influence over the direction of city government in Salem was second only to Hurley himself.

Although he did not know it at the time of his election, his political success would be the only positive of the period. His friend, Sullivan, had been on a number of celebrity tours since losing the title, so Jack was seeing much less of him. Occasionally he would stop in Salem and visit the Derby Street store. On rare occasions, Jack went into Boston to spend time with his uncle and the former champ. On these occasions, he couldn't help but feel bad as his old friend was no longer training, and it showed more and more each time they met. He was overweight and drinking a lot but still had the celebrity status that got him a great reception everywhere he went.

The bigger reason for trips into Boston was to meet with McGowan, Foley, his uncle, and other members of the Fenian Brotherhood to get status reports. British operatives were known to be working around Boston and New York with local officials to gain insight into the membership and operation of the Brotherhood. They had not caught them red-handed, but they knew guns had come out of New York as well as Boston. Two shipments of guns being brought in from Germany had been seized, much like the guns from Boston. The British were constantly on the lookout for gun shipments, wherever they were coming from. Pat McGowan had been questioned by them on several occasions. He, of course, was quick to point out to them that they had no authority in the United States, and if local authorities wanted to question him, they could speak to his attorney. He had the financial resources to protect himself with good legal counsel. This being the case, attempting to obtain any information from him was a waste of time. McGowan found the efforts amusing and would laugh out loud when telling the story of their visits.

McGowan remained the leader of the chapter of the Brotherhood, even in their state of inactivity. So the news of his death on November 30, 1896, was a devastating blow not only to the Brotherhood but to all that knew him. Pat had been tremendously successful in his life in spite of the anti-Irish sentiment he encountered upon landing in America in 1851. Over his forty-five years in the country, he amassed a large portfolio of properties in South Boston and left his four children a large fortune. With all he had overcome in his life, he could not overcome the massive heart attack that ended his life at seventy-one years of age. His business was taken over by his two sons and continued to grow and to provide financial support to the brotherhood. However, his leadership was lost and very much missed.

Jack, Tom, and their wives all attended a huge funeral in Boston. Pat Cashman's whole family attended, as did the former champ, as well as Jake Kilrain, who had become a friend of Sullivan and McGowan after the epic fight in '89. It was said to be the largest funeral in Boston up until that time. McGowan's friendships and business relationships reached into the highest levels of political and social life in Boston. He would always say that it was ironic how all the Boston Bramans who didn't want the Irish immigrants were quick to come around when you had money. It was not to be the last funeral Jack would be attending in the nineties.

That next year, Anna, who had not been feeling well for a number of months, was diagnosed with tuberculosis. The news was yet another severe blow to the McCarthy clan. Johanna had reached seventy years of age and had slowed noticeably. Anna's diagnosis left her shaken to her core. The two were always friendly as neighbors and had become close over the years of Anna's marriage to Jack. So close that as Anna's condition grew worse, so did Johanna's.

Jack tried to stay upbeat about it all, telling Anna, "We can beat this together. We can't let this beat us." A driver who refused to give in to adversity, he felt they could beat this illness.

Anna was far more realistic about the situation, telling Jack, "We have to be aware that I'm not going to be here to see the boys grow. This is not the common cold I have developed. It's a terminal illness."

In spite of her realism, Jack stayed in denial until her condition worsened to the point that even he had to face reality. He was getting help with the children from Anna's sister, Bridget, whom the boys called Aunt Veno. Bridget did not like her given name, so she had the boys call her by her chosen nickname. With Anna and Johanna putting in very little time at the store and Jack busy with city matters, Tom and Mary had taken on more help. Mary's sister, Dierdre, was now a full-time employee as was Anna's cousin, Sinead. The family was struggling to make the best of bad times. Then another blow hit.

On January 12, 1898, Uncle Pat dropped dead of a heart attack at age sixty-eight. His death was a shock as he had been working every day, seemingly healthy. The news devastated Johanna all the more as Pat was her younger brother. Jack had been charged with carrying the sad news to her. Johanna was in the home on Becket Street with Tom's three children as Jack came over from the store.

"Ma, can you sit with me here at the table so I can talk with you?"

"Please don't tell me Anna is worse. I know that I can't handle hearing of more suffering with that poor girl."

"No, Ma, it's not Anna." They both sat at the table. Johanna looked at her son's sad eyes. She knew what was coming would not be good, and her youngest son was struggling with the telling of it. This woman, who had endured so much suffering and hardship in her life, braced herself for yet another blow.

"You obviously have bad news, son, so you may as well come right out with it."

Jack let out a long sigh as he stared into his mother's eyes. This was going to be very hard for her. He hated to see her pain.

"Ma, Uncle Pat had a heart attack on the job this morning, and he died before they could get him to a hospital for help."

Johanna blessed herself saying, "Jesus, Mary, and Joseph, please give us strength. Is there no end to the tragedy that has beset us lately?" She shook all over as she digested the news while looking at her son.

Jack rose and went to his mother to embrace her as she broke down in tears. He held her until she was able to stop crying. She patted Jack's shoulder, telling him, "I need to say a rosary for my dear brother. May God take his soul to heaven. He was such a good man."

"Yes, he was, Ma. I'm sure he is with the Lord now."

"After I say a rosary, can you take me to the train station so I can go into Boston to be with Pat's family?"

"Yes, Ma, I will go over to the store to make sure Tom is all right, then I will go to Boston with you." Jack left his mother and went over to the store to talk with his brother.

Tom and Jack decided to close the store for the rest of the day. The two brothers, plus Johanna, arrived at Pat's house in Boston to find a large group of the family's friends already in attendance. Johanna went immediately to the side of Pat's widow, Barbara. They embraced in tears while Johanna said how sorry she was for the loss. Barbara, at sixty-seven years old, was not in the best of health herself. The loss of her husband so suddenly and unexpectedly had left her in shock.

Jack and Tom spent time with Pat's four children. The two oldest boys, James and John, had been working with their father for years. On this day, they were both on a separate job from Pat and not there when he fell. The youngest son, Conor, at age twenty-three, was working with his father when he collapsed. All three were devastated, but Conor, having witnessed it, was badly shaken by the tragedy. The McCarthy brothers did what they could to comfort all three boys, plus Dierdre, Pat's daughter.

The Irish accepted death as an inevitable part of life. Irish wakes were famous for their celebration of the life of the deceased. However, the sudden, completely unexpected death such as Pat's were the most difficult to deal with, and the three McCarthys, while offering comfort, were as devastated as everyone else in the house.

Another large Irish funeral in Boston, Anna was unable to make it. Jack sat with his mother, Tom, and Mary. Pat's widow, four children, their spouses, and eight grandchildren took up the first two pews. Pat's sons, James and John Cashman, took over what had been built up to a good size construction company. They changed the name to Cashman Brothers Construction and continued to grow the company long after Pat's death. The brothers branched out from a straight construction company, adding a barge business and eventually specializing in marine construction. The company, started by an Irish immigrant in 1860, would grow to be one of the largest and most respected construction companies in Massachusetts. Both James and John proved to be exceptional businessmen.

Back in Salem, while Jack's political career continued its success, Anna continued to lose strength. Jack and Johanna were spending more time taking care of her while her sister Bridget, alias Aunt Veno, was taking care of the boys more often.

One day speaking with his sister-in-law, Mary, Jack confided, "I can't stand to watch her deteriorate like this. Her beauty and spirit are all but gone. That fabulous sarcastic sense of humor is gone. She is a shell of her former self. The boys and I try to cheer her, but the entire apartment is troubled and saddened. I pray every night that it will turn around, but in my heart I know it won't."

"You can't give up hope, Jack, even if Anna has. Your strength is all she has left."

These words were small consolation to the grieving husband. On September 11, 1898, Father O'Leary from the Immaculate Conception Church was brought in to administer last rites as Anna Hennessey McCarthy gave up the ghost. All in the family knew it was coming, yet the impact was no less. Johanna broke down emotionally and physically. Jack and the boys were inconsolable. After crying over his dear wife's remains, giving her one last embrace, Jack walked out of the apartment alone. He disappeared for the rest of the day, leaving his ever supportive brother to work with Father O'Leary on the funeral arrangements. By nine that evening, he had not returned, so the family became concerned. They sent Tom out to find his brother. After several hours, he found him sitting on a stone wall overlooking Salem Harbor. Jack was holding what was left of a bottle of Irish whiskey purchased from Tim O'Shea's pub. He was very drunk.

"Jack, you need to come home now. Your boys and Ma have been very worried about you."

"I have lost her. I have lost the most lovely woman God ever created. I've lost the love of my life." He spoke in slurs, sniffles, and tears with his head hung low as he sat slouched over. Tom felt he had never seen a more pathetic human in his life.

"I know it's awful, Jack, but you must carry on for your boys and for yourself."

"I can't, Tom, I can't, I can't."

He collapsed into Tom's arms. Tom threw his brother over his shoulder and carried him back home, putting him to bed in his house so his two sons, who were in the apartment over the store with their aunt, Bridget, would not see him. He then went to his mother's room and up to the apartment to tell all that Jack was home safe. Johanna was glad he was home, but very concerned about her son's state of mind.

It seemed the entire Irish neighborhood, as well as a large group from Boston, turned out for Anna's funeral. At the young age of thirty-four years, her death was seen by all as a terrible tragedy. She had been a friend to all in the Irish neighborhood. They all mourned her loss. That beautiful smile and her famous sarcastic wit would be missed by all who knew her. She was a tender, loving presence in the Derby Street neighborhood.

After the funeral, Jack continued to drink heavily. He would start drinking in the store in midafternoon, then leave for O'Shea's as soon as the store closed, leaving the boys with their aunt.

In spite of encouraging talks from his bother stressing Jack's ongoing obligations, this behavior continued on for days. He missed several meetings at Salem City Hall, which drew the wrath of John Hurley, his political mentor. Hurley came to the store on September 23 to meet with Jack and Tom to encourage Jack to get back on track.

Nothing seemed to be having any effect on him as he continued the behavior of a man who had given up.

His bouts of drunken behavior were getting uglier at O'Shea's. Twice Tim himself had shut off a belligerent Jack who was argumentative and surly. Finally, on September 27, he got in a fist fight in the bar, breaking the nose of a fellow patron. O'Shea threw him out, banning him from returning for a month. This incident brought the wrath of someone much fiercer than John Hurley.

Jack was awakened the morning of September 28 by a sound slap in the face from his mother. She had just been informed of the events of the previous night, and Johanna McCarthy had seen enough.

"Jack, I'm so ashamed of you. I have spent the last hour crying in my room. I cannot believe a son of mine, a son of the John McCarthy I married, would be acting like the sniveling coward I see laying here in this bed. Do you think you are the first to lose a loved one? The first to bear tragedy? Your father, your Uncle Pat, and God himself are looking down at a coward who is not a man. A man would know he has a responsibility to his two sons, two sons that right now are ashamed of their father. A man would know he has a responsibility to his brother, a responsibility to the people that elected him. You just imagine how you would have turned out if I had acted this way when your father died. You get your Irish arse out of this bed, clean yourself up, and act like a man, or so help me, I will break your nose again myself. You stay away from the bottle, you carry on with your life, and you meet your responsibilities like a man, just as your father did, and his father did, and his father before him. Now get up."

A bleary-eyed hungover Jack McCarthy heard his mother's words and knew she was right. This woman had always been his best counsel since he was a small boy. Her wisdom he never questioned.

Get up he did, feeling totally ashamed of himself. On that day, he apologized to his brother, to Tim O'Shea, and all he had offended at the pub. He apologized to his fellow alderman and his customers. That night, he apologized to his sons, promising the two of them that he would never touch another drop of whiskey. To his dying day, he never did. He took the pledge he made to his sons to his grave, never again in his life having an alcoholic drink. His two sons, John and William, also never drank in their lives as they elected to follow their father's sobriety pledge.

The death of her brother and her daughter-in-law was apparently the final emotional straw for the seventy-three-year-old Johanna. She died of pneumonia on December 12, barely three months after Anna's death and three months after her life altering speech to her son, yet another funeral for the McCarthys. The entire family of her brother Pat made the trip from Boston as once again a large crowd was present at the funeral. A very tough, religious, and caring Irish woman, Johanna Cashman McCarthy was a beloved member of her church and community. Many mourned her loss, none more than her sons. A strong matriarch who raised her two boys alone with few financial resources, she never took a penny of help from anyone, choosing to earn her way and to make do with what she had. Her tough Irish independent attitude was admired by the entire neighborhood.

As the century came to a close, Jack McCarthy faced the world as a successful political figure in Salem, as well as a successful businessman with his brother Tom. He was now an orphan as both his parents were deceased. He had been left a widower at thirty-nine with two young boys. What he did have was the support of his deceased wife's family, particularly her sister, Bridget. He also had the support of his brother's family, as well as the entire neighborhood around Derby Street. He would face the new century with all that support, and he would continue to espouse the principles he felt in his heart, wherever those principles would lead. Issues in Ireland that remained unresolved also remained dear to his heart. His young cousin, Conor Cashman, shared those feelings as they both attended Fenian Brotherhood meetings. His two sons were growing fast, and he would never again shirk the responsibility he had to them. Much was left to be done. Jack McCarthy stood ready to do his part.

CHAPTER XV

History is full of examples of oppression of one class of people by another class. This has long been true in Ireland, where the oppression of a Catholic majority has lasted for centuries. Throughout the years of an Anglo-Irish privileged class, restrictions to access of institutional authority aimed at controlling the Catholic majority to the advantage of landowners highlighted the oppression of a majority by a minority. Without the ability to address grievances through legislative authority and without access to any means of creating wealth, the oppression by a minority was perpetuated. This was all made possible by the always present heavy hand of British authority.

In Ireland, the dissension caused by the unfair treatment of great masses of people erupted into periodic rebellions. The Catholic population, which made up the majority in Ireland, had long been oppressed, treated as second-class citizens not only because of religious bigotry but mainly for economic purposes to benefit the landed gentry. Every action had a reaction, so the oppression would result in rebellion, and rebellions would result in counter moves by the oppressors. The history of Ireland is a history of action bringing reaction with little or no change for centuries.

In the late eighteenth century, Ireland had its own parliament, albeit subservient to the English parliament. The desire for further independence from Britain as well as the push for Catholic emancipation brought about a rebellion in 1798. While supported by Britain's longtime rival, France, the rebellion was nonetheless crushed by the British in a bloody fashion. The idea that an emancipated Catholic majority in Ireland would bring about an alliance with an independent Ireland and France was a very troubling prospect for England and a prospect they intended to never see fulfilled.

With all this unrest boiling over, British Prime Minister William Pitt knew that action was needed to be taken to put things to rest, so he proposed the Act of Union in 1799, an act referred to by Byron as a "union of a shark and its prey." England had passed the Act of Union in 1707 that resulted in Scotland losing its own parliament to become part of the United Kingdom. The idea was to do the same thing with Ireland. The act had to be passed by both the English as well as the Irish parliaments. It took two tries and an estimated quarter of a million pounds sterling in bribes to pass the Irish parliament, but when it did, Ireland became part of the United Kingdom.

This action also caused a reaction as the Union was extremely unpopular with the oppressed majority in Ireland. Almost immediately, there was a drive to repeal the Act of Union. This movement took on momentum when Daniel O'Connell took up the cause. He was able to generate great support through petitions and well-attended public meetings. In spite of his great efforts throughout the 1830s, the parliament in London ignored him while the seat of power in Ireland, Dublin Castle, tolerated him. After a time, groups of his supporters became disillusioned with his approach. They formed a group called the Young Irelanders.

Leaders of this group like Thomas Davis, Charles Duffy, and John Blake Duffy proposed a much more aggressive approach to repeal. They started a national newspaper in 1842 with the purpose of inspiring new members to join the Young Irelanders. In 1848, this group organized its own armed rebellion. The main skirmish took place in Ballingar, County Typerary. Like the previous rebellions, it was crushed, and the leaders arrested. Some leaders like John Mitchel, William O'Brian, and Thomas Meapheir were banished to Van Diemons Land, Tasmania, Australia. Two leaders who escaped, James Stephens and John O'Mahony, would play a major role in future efforts.

All the frustrations, all the animosity, all the hatred toward Britain was dramatically intensified by the famine and the British *laissez-faire* response. All the suffering, all the deaths, not only intensified feelings in Ireland, the immigration of over a million Irish to America and elsewhere created a whole new problem for the British. Those immigrants carried the scars of the famine with them.

The Fenian movement literally grew out of the famine. James Stephens, who escaped to France after the Young Irelanders rebellion, came back to Ireland to form the Irish Republican Brotherhood (*Bvaithreachas Phoblacht n h Eirean*) in 1858. Another escapee from that rebellion, John O'Mahoney, founded the sister organization, the Fenian Brotherhood (*Clan Na Gael*) in America. Both of these organizations were dedicated to Irish independence. Members took an oath when they joined to swear dedication to the cause. The oaths went through several iterations, but all the versions were basically the same:

> In the presence of God, I... do solemnly swear that I will do my utmost to establish independence of Ireland, and that I will bear true allegiance to the Supreme Council of the Irish Republican Brotherhood and the Government of the Irish Republic and implicitly obey the constitution of the Irish Republican Brotherhood and all my superior officers and th...at I will preserve inviolable the secrets of the organization.

The American organizations funded much of the activity in Ireland. They were active in recruiting Irish immigrants who fought in the Civil War to form an army for a planned five-prong attack on the British holdings in North America, namely, Canada. The plan was to occupy Canadian cities then trade the release for an independent Ireland. Short of the trade, they hoped to at least require the British to send troops to defend Canada, leaving Ireland more vulnerable to an insurrection.

This failed, as did the Fenian Rebellion. On March 5, 1867, thousands of Fenians marched from Dublin to Tallaght. The march was a decoy to draw British troops out of Dublin in advance of attacks. This march was coordinated with attacks on a string of constabulary barracks in places like Dundrum, as well as in Cork and Dublin. Just as in the case of the Canadian attack, the effort failed, at least partly because informants in the ranks let the British know the plans in advance and partly because of poor communication.

In any event, the two organizations did not go away after these failures. For a time, they worked in conjunction with the efforts for home rule. However, this movement was always seen by the Brotherhood as a means to an end, not the end. The end result they wanted was independence.

The IRB was behind a number of plots and bombings in the last two decades of the century. Much of the activity in the "dynamite campaign" drew a backlash of resentment against the organization. A bombing at the Clerkinwell Prison in London that killed twelve innocent neighbors is a good example. In what became known as the Phoenix Park Murders, the IRB killed the chief secretary for Ireland Lord Cavendish and his secretary. These activities were less effective than planned while at the same time causing a backlash against the entire movement.

This is where things stood as the nineteenth century came to a close. The London Metropolitan Police had formed a special Irish branch to deal with the IRB. Similarly, the British Consulate in America had a unit with the same charge in respect to the Fenian Brotherhood. The IRB had lost some of its steam and was a weakened organization by 1900. Still, the push for independence would continue, while the resistance from the United Kingdom to do everything in their power to prevent its success would also continue.

In Salem, Massachusetts, far across the ocean from this troubled land, Jack McCarthy would continue his own efforts to assist the cause. In spite of personal tragedies, responsibilities to family, business, and local government, his dedication to the cause would not waiver. While Pat McGowan, Pat Cashman, and Peter Grady were gone, Jack had picked up an ally in his cousin, Conor Cashman, who shared the same dedication. Both were members of the Fenian Brotherhood in Boston. By 1902, Conor had become the president of the Brotherhood, a position formerly held by Pat McGowan. At the tender age of twenty-seven, Conor was both a very young and very enthusiastic leader intent on reviving an organization that had become weakened by the deaths of its leaders. Things were changing in Ireland, and both Jack and Conor wanted to be a part of the change. The first step would be to bring the Boston chapter of the Fenian Brotherhood back to its former status.

CHAPTER XVI

On February 10, 1902, the Fenian Brotherhood met in Boston, with Conor Cashman running the meeting. Since the death of Pat McGowan and the seizing of the gun shipment, the group had been laying low. Meanwhile the British Navy had seized gun shipments from New York, just as they did the Boston shipment. It had become apparent that the Brits were tightening their control, so further shipments would be a huge risk.

The meeting was attended by only twenty-three members, in addition to Conor. Jack was there to support his cousin, but meetings that used to involve upward of a hundred members had shrunk down to this size.

The intention of Cashman was to revive the Brotherhood. He opened the meeting by letting it be known, "We need to bring this organization back into a place where we are relevant. Otherwise, what's the point of us meeting? Our fellow Irish are in a life struggle for independence, and we need to be on the team." His speech went on about the important role they could be playing instead of being intimidated by British attempts to limit their activity.

"I am personally heading to Ireland next month to try to arrange meetings with the leadership of the IRB. I intend to find out what they need from us at this point, then come back here to get us busy bringing in new members and providing whatever support they tell me they need from us." The members present were all in support of this initiative. Cashman intended to bring Dan Foley, Pat McGowan's good friend, with him because Foley had accompanied McGowan in the last visit with IRB leadership. After a bit more discussion, it was agreed to take money from the treasury to send the two over to Ireland in March. What's more, it was further agreed to solicit donations from businesses and individuals, so the two did not have to go over empty-handed. Members weren't sure exactly what was needed by the IRB, but they knew that money always helped.

After the meeting broke up, Conor went out for a drink with his cousin, Jack.

"Conor, I think what you are planning is the right thing to do. Tom and I will contribute money from the store. If it were not for my two boys, I might even go with you. But having said all that, be very careful over there. I already lost my best friend to this cause. I don't want to lose my cousin."

"I'm not blind to the dangers, Jack. I know we need to move forward on both sides of the Atlantic. I intend to do what I can to push things along on both sides."

"I understand all that, Conor, just be aware that the Brits are on their toes on both sides of the Ocean. Don't end up in one of their prison cells."

"I will be careful not to let that happen. I appreciate your willingness to contribute. I know my brothers will kick in, as well as McGowan's company, so we should be able to make a good contribution to the cause."

"Well, before you go, come up to Salem to spend the night with Tom and me and the kids. They would love to see you."

They parted company with Conor promising to spend a night in Salem before he left. Jack took the train home, arriving in time to relieve his sister-in-law Bridget from her babysitting duties. His boys had now been three and a half years without their mother. They had spent a lot of that time with Bridget, a.k.a. Aunt Veno. She had become a surrogate mother to the boys as she spent much of her time with them when she was not working at her job. Both John and William loved their "Aunt Veno." They relied on her tremendously. She had been there for them to help heal the wounds after the deaths of their mother and grandmother.

Jack, three and a half years without his wife, had chosen to bury himself in his work at the store, at city hall, as well as looking after

John and Bill. He had not shown any interest in another woman since Anna's death even though several had shown an interest in him.

Bridget, while quite attractive, had never married, although she came very close a few years after Jack had married Anna. Jack very much appreciated her help with the boys. The two of them had always gotten along well as in-laws. While always friends, neither could ever picture a relationship beyond friendship. They both harbored the same feelings that anything beyond friendship would be a betrayal of Anna. So Jack arrived home to once again thank her for taking care of the boys. She gave a report of their good behavior before retiring to her parents' home across the street. They would both sleep alone that night, as well as many other nights, rather than bear the burden of betraying the departed Anna.

Conor kept his promise to spend a night in Salem before departing for Ireland. He came up on March 12 to join Jack, Tom, Mary, and the five kids for dinner at Tom's Becket Street home. While Mary fixed an Irish stew with soda bread feast, the five children spent time with the three men. Jack's oldest, John, had developed into a fine piano player, so he played while the rest of the crew sang along. After dinner, the adults shared drinks, discussing a number of topics, including the ever-expanding business reach of Cashman Brothers Construction. Conor worked with his two brothers, John and James, in building what had become the number-one construction company in Boston. His two brothers had both married and had been blessed with two children each. Conor, the biggest of the three brothers at six feet three inches and 190 pounds, had developed a well-earned reputation around Boston as a lady's man. He had no intention of marrying. As he would say, he was having too much fun to settle into a marriage. His two older brothers were absolutely dedicated to building the business their father had left them. McCarthy Brothers Store and Lunch Counter also enjoyed continued business success. Jack's additional duties in his political career also went well. He was becoming ever more influential in the Salem community.

Eventually the talk turned to the upcoming trip to Ireland. Conor told them he was proud of the Cashman Brothers success. It was a lasting legacy to his father, Pat, and he worked hard for the company. But he was not as wedded to it as his two brothers. His commitment to an independent Ireland was his main purpose in life as he saw things. While they admired his dedication to a cause they all supported, the McCarthys all worried for Conor's safety.

Mary and Tom both echoed Jack's sentiment that Conor should be careful over there. They all told him they would be praying for his safe return. He stayed that night at Tom's house, leaving the next day after spending some time in the store the next morning. As he left, the McCarthys were all thinking that this was how Peter Grady had left the last time they ever saw him.

CHAPTER XVII

In Ireland, much like in Boston, a new group of leaders had taken over the Irish Republican Brotherhood. Bulmer Hobson, Dennis McCullough, and Sean MacDiarmada were as intent on revitalizing the IRB as Cashman was intent on revitalizing the Fenian Brotherhood in Boston. They were joined by Thomas Clark, who had been released after fifteen years in jail as punishment for his Fenian activities. Clark and MacDiarmada were intent on attracting new recruits to build the movement back up.

The ship carrying Cashman and Foley to Ireland set sail on March 20, arriving in Cobh Harbor in early April. Through older contacts from past trips, Foley arranged a meeting in Dublin with Hobson and McCullough. They met at O'Donald's pub on O'Connel Street, and they huddled in a snug with pints of Guinness, while greetings were passed around. Conor explained that he was the new president of the Boston Chapter of the Brotherhood and that it was his intention to bring it back to its former prominence under Pat McGowan. "And as a token of that commitment I'm pleased to present the IRB with two thousand US dollars to help with your efforts."

The two leaders thanked them for the contribution. They commented that they appreciated the commitment. They all remembered well the great friend they had in Pat McGowan. "It's great to see that a young enthusiastic Irishman has taken up the banner to continue his work."

"Well, the whole purpose of my trip here is to get a feel for how things are over here. Particularly I need to learn specifically what we can do to be more helpful." Hobson went into an explanation of how the failed revolts as well as the "dynamite campaign" had resulted in the IRB losing favor with some of the population. They had been weakened, and the membership was down. On the plus side, there had been developments that were very positive in reviving the Irish spirit. The Gaelic League started in the 1890s with the aim of promoting the Irish language as well as the Irish culture in general. The Gaelic Athletic Association also started in the nineties to promote Irish games and the health of Irish people. The Irish National Literary Society started by W. B. Yeats was yet another organization to promote Irish culture.

"Our spirit has been on the decline, Conor, ever since the great hunger. These movements have helped to revive that spirit. We at the IRB have used these organizations to help us recruit new members by showing that preserving Irish culture and health can only be protected by providing an independent Ireland."

"The key question I need answered for now is, what are the plans over the next few years and how can we contribute?" Conor asked.

This question brought a lengthy response from the two leaders. They had two major immediate objectives. First, they needed to rebuild their membership and re-establish their cause in the hearts and minds of the Irish people. To do this they had assigned two of their high-ranking members, Sean MacDiarmada and Thomas Clark, to recruit new members. The two were working in conjunction with the Gaelic Athletic League and the Gaelic League, as mentioned before. In addition, they had a number of longer-term initiatives. They intended to start a newspaper called *Irish Freedom* in order to tell their story in print on a regular basis, in order to offset British propaganda. They had plans to start a youth organization, *Nq Fianna Eiveann*, to encourage young people to study their heritage and culture. They wanted to establish a sense of nationalism in the next generation so they knew what was being fought to achieve. Younger Irish did not experience the famine, did not appreciate the British response to the famine. They needed to know what independence would mean and why it was essential.

Second, they intended to get busy again building for another insurrection. The Unionist in Ulster were against home rule as well as any talk of independence. The Unionists had begun to organize militarily with volunteer units. The IRB needed to offset this with volunteer units of their own in Ulster. They were moving to build up the Irish volunteers. The gun shipment seizures in recent years had hindered both recruitment and training.

"What has changed that would make you think it's going to be any easier to get ammunitions into your hands?" Conor asked.

"It will always be difficult, but the British are in the beginnings of an arms race with Germany. Their attention is focused on Germany for a number of reasons. Plus they are working on forming an alliance with a longtime enemy, France, because of their concerns with Germany. We are counting on their guard being down."

"Do you want us to work on another arms shipment?"

"No, we are more able to receive arms from Germany. The Germans are better equipped to complete arms shipments. What we need to meet all of these objectives is more of what you just delivered."

Conor nodded his understanding, and instructions were given on the best way to get money to the right people. Hobson suggested that they meet the next morning in the lobby at Conor's hotel so that he could take the two Americans to a training facility. Conor agreed, so they left the pub and walked down O'Connel Street. Hobson said he wanted to show them the root of the problem. They walked all the way to Dublin Castle, stopping across the street. Hobson pointed and said, "There stands the seat of power in Ireland today, Dublin Castle. They make all the rules, all the laws, right there. We, the Irish people, have no say in who occupies this seat of power. We have no say on the rulings they make, and no power to change them. That is the problem we face."

The next morning, Cashman and Foley were picked up at their hotel and driven by carriage to a location two hours outside Dublin. At a very rural farm, they were introduced to half-dozen members of the volunteer force. They walked them through a field where maneuvers were held twice a month with the local volunteer force, including target shooting. After the walk through the field, they were shown a weapons cachet hidden under a concealed trap door in the barn. The rifles were a collection of mismatched firearms. About half were fairly new, with some of the others so old, Conor felt they probably didn't even fire.

"We have to keep these hidden to avoid seizure. We only have sixty-three weapons here, so we have to bring volunteers here in groups because we do not have enough weapons to go around," Hobson explained.

"Are the training sessions known to the British?"

"We have to post guards when there are maneuvers planned. We also switch them from place to place to avoid detection. We have no illusions that our forces will be as well trained as the opposition forces. We are just hoping to do the best we can to get them ready."

Cashman left the location concerned that the facilities, the equipment, indeed the entire operation, was inadequate. When they returned to Dublin, Cashman suggested a dinner meeting for later that evening because he wanted an opportunity to speak to Foley before the meeting. When they were alone, Cashman explained his concerns. "Dan, there needs to be some effort on our side to somehow assist with preparing a force."

"What do you have in mind, Conor? I mean there is an ocean between us."

"Agreed, but we have good Irishmen in the US who have served in the military. Perhaps there is a way to sponsor them to come to Ireland to help with training. Also, perhaps offer the service of some of these trained soldiers to join in when the insurrection begins."

Foley reflected on this for a moment before responding, "That's a lot to ask, Conor, a very difficult assignment to pull off."

"Well, I'm going to suggest something along these lines over dinner. Perhaps they can add some meat to the bones."

He did propose this level of cooperation over dinner. The proposal was met with skeptical appreciation, with Hobson pointing out the same pitfalls to the proposal that Foley had pointed out. They hashed it over for the duration of the dinner and after-dinner drinks. The final result was that both sides would consider some arrangement of the type Cashman proposed with the members of their leadership and that they would keep lines of communication open.

Before leaving to go back to Boston, Conor Cashman traveled by train to Cork City to meet with his cousins from his father's side. It had been fifteen years since his cousin Jack had visited. Amazingly, his Uncle Sean and Aunt Grainne were still alive, as were all nine of their children. The nineteen grandchildren had expanded to twenty-three plus two great grandchildren from Sean Jr.'s oldest child, Sinead. As with his cousin Jack, they all got together at Sean's farm in Killy Donohue for a huge feast. Sean was now in his midseventies as was Grainne, but both were in good health. The entire assemblage said a joint prayer for their departed loved ones, Patrick and Johanna. Following that somber moment, the food and drink flowed, as well as music and conversation. They were all interested in the success of Cashman Brothers Construction. A couple of the boys, Eamon and Jay, both in their early twenties, asked about the chances of them coming to America to work for the company. Conor promised to make that a priority project when he returned home. "You can't have enough Cashmans around," he commented to laughter and applause.

Conor was also encouraged to find that several of the Cashman boys were proud members of the Irish Republican Brotherhood. Sean Jr., now in his midforties, was friendly with Bulmer Hobson, so he suggested Conor send any correspondence intended for the officers of the IRB to Sean first. He would make sure it got to the proper people. Conor promised to keep them informed on activities in America with the brotherhood. They promised to reciprocate. Conor told them all that his brothers, James and John, both planned on coming over with their families. He was assured that they would receive a warm welcome home.

It was all so enjoyable that Conor stayed at the farm for three days before joining Dan Foley in Cork City to begin the journey home. They sailed from Cobh Harbor with Conor bursting at the seams to report home to the Fenian Brotherhood.

CHAPTER XVIII

Upon his return to Boston, Conor filled in his brothers and sister and their families with the details of the visit with the relatives across the pond. Both James and John intended to bring their families over to meet these same relatives, so they were keenly interested in the details. Conor wanted to immediately pursue the idea of having their two cousins, Jay and Eamon, come to America to work at Cashman Brothers Construction. His brothers agreed. As important as these family and business matters were, Conor couldn't wait to get up to Salem to talk with his cousin about his meeting with Hobson.

Two days after returning to Boston, he headed to Salem. He wanted the advice of his cousin who had been involved in the struggle longer than he had been, his cousin whom he had always looked up to as a man who gave thoughtful sound advice.

He desperately wanted to take the proper action here to be as supportive of the drive for independence as he possible could be from his side of the Atlantic.

He showed up at the store just before closing with an eye towards spending the night with the McCarthys. Jack was not in the store at the time, but Tom and Mary welcomed him with open arms. They both were thankful to see him home safe and sound.

"Can't wait to hear the details of your trip, Conor. I know Jack will feel the same. Of course, you'll stay for the night."

"I would love to, Tom, if I'm not intruding."

"Nonsense, you know you are always welcome."

Some of the locals asked Conor questions about his stay in Ireland. They had heard about the continuing push for independence. He was glad to answer their questions and discuss the Irish situation. He sat for over an hour filling the locals with stories of the Irish push for independence.

Tom closed up the store and ushered Conor into his Becket Street home. Mary was as happy to see him as Tom. "Of course, you will join us for dinner?"

"Would you have enough, Mary? I've arrived unannounced."

"Just another potato in the pot, Conor. In fact, Tom, send John up to get Jack and the two boys."

Tom took on the task himself, coming back a few minutes later with the three McCarthys from the apartment. Upon their arrival, Mary received help from her daughters, Margaret and Molly, to finish fixing a dinner for all while Jack's son John played the piano, and Tom broke out drinks for the men, except Jack, who kept his pledge. The festivities and the dinner lasted until after nine, when the five younger McCarthys were sent to prepare their work for school the next day.

"They are growing up fast. Are they all in their teens now?" Conor asked.

Mary answered, "All but Bill. He's twelve, so only a year away. We have them all working in the store now in their spare moments."

"Jack, I think John is old enough to work this summer for the construction company, if he would like."

"Wow, I will have to talk to him about that tomorrow, but for now, let's hear about your meeting with the IRB."

Conor had relayed the stories of his time with the Cashman relatives while the whole family was at the dinner table. He saved the details of his meeting with Hobson and McCullogh until it was just the three adults.

He explained the work going on to preserve the culture and restore the spirit of the Irish people. He felt the organizations created to accomplish those objectives, the Gaelic League and the Gaelic Athletic Association, were moving things in the right direction. The efforts to recruit new members were also gaining steam. He went into some detail about the money that was needed to bring success to these initiatives.

As he began to transition to the military initiatives, Jack spoke up, "I'm sure the money is both essential and in short supply, but with our declining membership, I don't know how helpful we can be now." Jack was thinking solely of the Boston Chapter of the Fenian Brotherhood. Conor had bigger aspirations.

"Money is the key, Jack, but not the only need. Their training facilities are rather rudimentary, also. Their supply of weapons is inadequate. They don't have the experienced military personnel to train the volunteers, plus they lack the resources to equip them if they do get them trained."

"I'm not sure how we can help address either need. We have problems of our own over here."

"That's why I'm here, Jack. I need your help to come up with some major initiatives to put us back on our feet so we can help our brothers over there."

With that, they began exploring different ideas around recruiting new members to the Fenian Brotherhood, and to finding experienced military personnel of Irish descent in America that could travel to Ireland to assist in training. Both Tom and Jack felt it would be extremely difficult to find US military retirees who would be willing to go over to Ireland to assist in training. What's more, if they were to raise a significant amount of money, Conor pointed out, it would have to involve more than the Boston chapter of the brotherhood.

"What might be helpful is to have some star power in our efforts to raise money," Conor offered.

"What do you have in mind?"

"How about your friend, Sullivan? He's not the champ anymore, but he still has plenty of star power."

"He has expressed support on a number of occasions," Tom added.

Jack reflected on the idea for a moment. "I can talk to him about it, but I'm not sure he would be willing to be the primary spokesman for the effort."

The conversation drifted back to the idea of finding retired military personnel for training assistance. Jack and Tom again felt it was a lot to ask to have someone leave their work and family to spend time in Ireland to train volunteers. After several hours of discussion, it was Mary who offered the best idea for a path forward.

"Why not have a couple of the members of the IRB Board come over to America to tour the east coast for the purpose of raising money. You could get John L. involved in some cities if he's available, but the main spokesmen would be the gentlemen from Ireland."

This suggestion was immediately and enthusiastically built upon by the three men. Conor said, "That's a brilliant suggestion. It will also help us in our efforts to recruit new blood. Having a couple of Irishmen involved on the front line of the struggle speak to a meeting of the Fenians would be a great tool in our recruitment."

Jack added, "Perhaps if we suggest that one of the visiting group be a leader in the military planning, we can also address your idea of using American military retirees to assist in the training."

Mary's suggestion started an avalanche of ideas on how to pull an effective visit together in terms of who should come, as well as where they go once they arrived. In the end, it was decided that Conor would send a letter to Bulmer Hobson, channeling it through their cousins Jay and Sean Cashman. In the letter, they would suggest that Hobson and Thomas Clark would come to America to spend two to four weeks raising money in the major cities on the east coast. Jack would approach John L. to see if he would assist by appearing with the travel group when possible. At meetings of the Fenian Brotherhood in these cities, Clark—being the major figure in the effort to recruit, arm, and train volunteers—would spell out the need for experienced personnel to see what kind of interest he could generate. As the evening wore on, the four of them jointly drafted the letter while they continued to excitedly throw out additional suggestions.

By two the following morning, their work completed, they all retired for the evening pleased with the results. Conor would post the letter in the morning as he headed back to Boston. At breakfast the next morning, a bleary-eyed group sent the youngest McCarthys off to school and Conor off to Boston. As tired as they all were, they were also excited about the prospect of their initiative being successful.

CHAPTER XIX

While they awaited response to their letter, Jack continued to tend to business at the store and at city hall. He had been appointed the chair of the finance committee, a position considered the second most powerful in Salem city government, second only to the mayor. His committee was responsible for putting together the annual municipal budget and to submit it for approval, in addition to the more mundane duties around building inspections, personnel issues, and citizen complaints.

At home, he had two boys growing up fast. John, at fourteen, had been offered a job for the summer working in Boston for Cashman Brothers Construction. He was so excited about this possibility that Jack had to be constantly on him to tend to his studies until the school year was over. Bill, at age twelve, was still content to work at the store, but he would constantly remind his father that in two years, he expected to follow his brother to work in construction. The excitement of working in Boston on a construction site, coupled with the fact that it paid so well, made for an irresistible combination.

One evening, after closing the store, Jack went upstairs to his apartment where Bridget was sitting at the kitchen table helping Bill with his homework.

"I don't know, Jack, I do the best I can with him," she said with wink and a smile.

"Come on, I'm doing okay here," Bill said with a bit of a wince.

"Well, I suppose you are, given what you have to work with," this coming out with a love tap on his arm. Bridget had a bit of the same sarcastic sense of humor as her sister, Anna.

"With you helping him like you do, how can he possibly fail?" Jack added.

"All right, I've taken enough. I'm going in with my brother." And with that, Bill left the room.

"Brid, why don't you join us for dinner? It's nothing special, I'm just heating up some stew."

"As appetizing as you make that sound, Jack, I think I will pass. There's a better offer waiting across the street."

"Listen, I really appreciate the time you spend with the boys. I don't know what I would do without you, and neither do the two of them. They love you. They depend on you, and they appreciate you tremendously."

They locked eyes for a long minute while Bridget tried to think of her response.

"I enjoy the two of them. They miss Anna terribly. I expect I'm the closest thing to her in their minds."

Jack thought as they looked at each other that she was indeed the closest thing to Anna in more ways than one. He looked away, breaking the long look between them. "They see you as a surrogate mother, Brid. You mean a lot to them."

"They mean a lot to me too, Jack."

"You mean a lot to all of us."

He looked back and found her still looking at him. The thought occurred to him, not for the first time, that there was a growing sexual tension between them. "Well again, thank you for all you do."

"Not to mention it," she said as she turned back to the door and made her exit. Jack stood looking after her until he noticed he was not alone in the room. His son, John, stood in the doorway from the living room. At fourteen, he was old enough to understand the interaction between his father and his aunt.

"You know, Pa, Bill and I both think it would be nice to have Aunt Veno around all the time."

Jack looked at his oldest son for a long moment before answering, "Do you really think this is your business, John?"

"I think our family is my business."

"You think it's time to replace your Ma?"

"Nobody will ever replace Ma with any of the three of us. We both know that. But living the rest of your life alone won't bring her back, Da."

"You're a smart young man, John. But you're not smart enough to understand what goes on inside my head and my heart. I hardly understand it myself."

"I don't pretend to, Da. I'm just telling you how Bill and I feel."

"I thank you for that, son, but it's more my issue to deal with."

With that, Jack went about fixing dinner for the three of them. His son sat down at the kitchen table contemplating their discussion. Not a word was spoken between them as dinner was being prepared. Finally, as Jack was dishing out the stew into three bowls, his son gave his final word, "We don't have to talk about it anymore, Da. Just know that Bill and I will be happy with any decision that makes you happy."

Jack looked over at his son and noticed that there were tears in his eyes. "I thank you for that, son." With that, he went about serving dinner.

Later that night, as he lay in bed staring at the ceiling, Jack reflected on the conversation he had with his son. There was little doubt that feelings had developed between him and Bridget that went beyond their longtime friendship. The question was would it be a betrayal of Anna if he pursued a relationship with her sister? Did he want a life companion or would it always be Anna he loved and wanted and would that be fair to Bridget? He finally fell asleep early in the morning with these thoughts running through his mind. He awoke the next morning still thinking of the situation and no closer to any decision.

Across Derby Street, Bridget had been wrestling all night with the same issues. She had no one to confide in, so she was left on her own in trying to deal with her feelings. Like Jack, she woke in the morning still troubled and no closer to a decision. The two adults were wrestling with this very difficult decision while the two younger McCarthys had already made up their minds.

CHAPTER XX

The letter from America was hand-delivered by Sean Cashman to Bulmer Hobson in Dublin. Hobson was about to leave by train to join his fellow Republican, Denis McCullough, in Belfast. He took the time to read the letter while Cashman sat with him having tea in a Dublin café. Finishing his reading, he reflected on the messages for a moment before addressing the courier. He did not want to reveal how excited the prospect of raising money in America had made him until he had thought it through.

"This is a very generous and timely suggestion from you cousin in America. We have a number of initiatives in very early stages that need money if we are to carry on with them. We are, in fact, in desperate need of money."

Sean nodded his understanding then responded, "I know that Conor and the rest of my family in America is anxious to help."

"I will let you know what we decide, and if we decide to go over, I will let you know the schedule. My first thought is that we will want to take advantage of this, so expect a positive response."

With that, they parted company. Sean headed for Cork; Hobson headed for Belfast. In Cork, Sean gave the details of his meeting to his younger brother, Jay, his mother, and his father. He had decided on the train ride back that if Hobson and company headed to America, then Eamon and Jay should go with them to take up cousin Conor's suggestion that they come over to work for Cashman Brothers. Jay was excited about the idea. Sean Sr. thought it was a great opportunity for both of his sons.

"Ireland is a poor country. Your futures would be much brighter in America, especially with the opportunity to work in the business run by your own family."

Their mother, Sinead, was less enthusiastic but still supportive. "I cannot imagine my life without you boys around, but your father is right. There is little opportunity here. I will miss you terribly, but I would never stand in your way." All this was spoken with tears in her eyes. Further discussion centered around planning the trip to America. In the end, it was decided that they shouldn't wait until Hobson and company went over.

Jay said, "If they ask us to post the response, Eamon and I should hand-deliver it, rather than post it."

With that, the Cashmans waited to hear from Hobson.

In Belfast, Hobson presented the letter to McCullough and sat quietly while he read.

With a broad smile after reading, McCullough said, "This is a great opportunity. We have such a need for money, this may be our guardian angel sending help."

The two patriots had each became somewhat disillusioned by the slow progress of the various organizations that pushed for independence. McCullough was particularly frustrated with the lack of activity of the IRB. Hobson was an early supporter of Arthur Griffith's *Cumann na n Gaedheal,* an organization formed to unite nationalist groups and clubs. They had jointly decided that it was past time for a more proactive approach. They planned to form Dungannon Clubs first in Ulster and later throughout Ireland. The name was taken from the 1782 volunteer convention at Dungannon, County Tyrone. The purpose was to promote Irish culture, Irish language, economic independence, and self-sufficiency for Ireland. Hobson planned to print a pamphlet with the Dungannon Clubs manifesto, which he and McCullough had written. The manifesto read in part:

> It is only with free political institutions that a
> people can develop its genius or its power; and so
> at the back of every evil that infests this land, over
> and above them all, and responsible for all, is the

government of Ireland by England. England governs this country against the wishes of its people.
Ethically her occupation of Ireland is immoral
and indefensible—but John Bull is not worried
with points of ethics or conscience. But so long as
he governs this land against the will of its people,
he has got to expect the utmost opposition from
the people he insists on governing. In the struggle between the two nations, our opponents have
got an efficient weapon of attack in the form of
the Government. We on the other hand have no
organization to oppose to their Government,
so we must create one as speedily as it may be.
England may not recognize it as representative of
the people, but her recognition is of little importance. A national organization that is going to
cope with injustice established for such a length
of time and so…

Further pamphlets would be produced and distributed.
Eventually they planned a weekly paper. All this was intended to
fast-track the recruitment into the IRB as well as to win the support
of all the Irish people to the cause of an independent Ireland.

Hobson told his partner he felt the same way about the opportunity. "This can be a great catalyst to the ends we seek, Denis. But
we have to plan it right. I thought about this all the way from Dublin.
I think we should answer in the affirmative, thank them for the offer,
but lay out what we need to make it worth our while."

"You have obviously thought through what you feel will make
it work our while."

"Yes I have, we need to ask them to draw up a schedule that
gets us to all the major cities, not just New York and Boston. I want
to speak to Fenian Brotherhood groups in Baltimore, Cincinnati,
Chicago, all the major cities, even if takes a month or more."

"So are you planning on you and me making this trip?"

"I am. They suggested in their letter that it be me and Tom Clark. We can certainly go with Tom, but you should come as well."

The two agreed to draft a response that included the request for a pre-arranged schedule. They would get the response back to Sean Cashman in Cork in order to keep him informed and also to protect against any British interference with the mailing. Both Hobson and McCullough were under the constant surveillance of British authority.

Once the response was delivered, they would await word from America as to the schedule of meetings before they made travel plans. The enthusiasm on the Ireland side of the Atlantic for this trip was as high as it was in America. They needed money to reach their goals. The best place to raise money was America. The Fenian Brotherhood groups in the major US cities were filled with Irish Americans that had done well financially in the adopted country. They were not so far removed from the famine years that their anti-British sentiments had faded. They were anxious to help, and they had the resources to provide that help. This could be a real catalyst to the cause of freedom.

CHAPTER XXI

The response from Ireland came in late August of 1903 with two Cashmans attached. Eamon and Jay arrived at the home of Conor Cashman in Boston, letter in hand, at eight thirty in the evening, to the surprise of Conor Cashman. After the initial shock wore off, Conor had them come in, giving them both a generous slug of Irish whiskey after their long journey.

"You two are certainly full of surprises. I can't wait to see the look on my brothers' faces when I show up at work tomorrow with you two."

"Shouldn't we announce our arrival?" asked Jay.

"Hell no, you nearly gave me a heart attack. I will not be letting the two of them off the hook."

They all settled in while Conor read the response. Having completed reading the letter, Conor pumped his fist in the air, yelling out his excitement. "Now we can really put together something that will make its mark on the uprising. Tomorrow night, we will have to go up to Salem to see your cousins, Jack and Tom, to give them the news. Oh, hell, I can't wait. I'm going to call Salem right now."

Telephones were a relatively new tool in the Boston area. Both the Boston Cashmans and the Salem McCarthys were early subscribers.

Conor got on the telephone to Jack to give him the good news. They were both so excited by the letter that Conor almost neglected to mention the two arrivals. When Jack suggested that Conor should come to Salem with the letter the following night, it jarred Conor's memory.

"Do you mind if I bring a couple of friends?"

"I suppose not, but who might your friends be?"

"Well, I have two dim-witted Irish chaps staying with me tonight named Eamon and Jay Cashman."

"Conor, you're joking. Have they just arrived in America?"

"Yes, they have. Tomorrow morning, I'm bringing them to the jobsite of a project here in Boston to meet me brothers. I think we may be able to give them a job, the company is quite busy right now. Once we sort out those details, we can head up to Salem."

Jack insisted that all three Cashmans spend the night, promising a good time would be had by all. The plans were set, so Jack headed over to Tom's house to set things in motion so that a meal, drinks, and a festive evening would be ready for the following night.

Tom and Mary were excited by the news and anxious to greet their cousins, as were all five McCarthy children. Mary made plans for the meal, while Tom and Jack discussed the letter that came with their cousins.

The next morning, Conor brought the two visiting Cashmans to a Boston jobsite being run by his brother, James. He had thought he would find both brothers there, but John had moved over to a project on the waterfront. James was suitably surprised at the arrival of his two cousins.

"You boys just arrived here last night. You must be exhausted."

"Ah, they are young boys, James, both in their twenties, they don't yet know what it means to be tired," Conor observed. Eamon and Jay confirmed that they were ready to go to work immediately, with plenty of energy.

"So you'd be looking for work, would ya?"

Jay spoke up, "Yes, sir, we would be good, loyal, hardworking men for you in whatever job you wanted us to do."

James was impressed with the enthusiasm expressed in the response. "Well, at the moment we have three projects going here in Boston, and four more in towns outside the city, so I think we can find you a place to work. Why don't we all get together at my house this evening when brother John is there. We can discuss with him the jobs we have going to decide where you would be needed."

Conor spoke, "Not tonight, brother. I'm taking the boys up to Salem to meet with Jack on a matter of importance to the Brotherhood." James was well aware of Conor's dedication to the Brotherhood.

James nodded, "All right then, tomorrow night at my house with John. Saturday night will work better anyway. There will not be work duties on Sunday. Here, take a walk with me boys, and I'll show you what we are doing here renovating this brownstone."

They walked through the oversize apartment building, which was completely torn apart as they prepared it for a total rehabilitation. James asked questions of the two boys, trying to get a feel for their work experience and their skill set. The two boys had worked as farm laborers. They had very little experience in the building profession. There would need to be a good deal of on-the-job training.

After a full tour of the project, James summed things up. "Tomorrow night, you meet the rest of your relatives while we review the projects we have going, so we can figure out where we put you two."

Eamon responded, "Wherever you want us to work, we will be ready." Jay quickly agreed with his brother.

Conor explained that he would have to be departing with the two boys, so they all shook hands and agreed to get together the following night.

Conor and the two boys caught the train to Salem, arriving at McCarthy Brothers store midafternoon. The McCarthys were all excited to meet their Irish cousins. After introductions were made and a quick tour of the store and living quarters, Tom and Jack took the three Cashmans down to O'Shea's for a drink, leaving the store in the capable hands of Mary and three of the young McCarthys. The two visitors were surprised when their cousin, Jack, ordered a cup of coffee. Conor later explained to them that Jack no longer drank. He did not get into details, and they didn't ask.

They brought the letter with them for Jack and Tom to read. Before the first round of drinks were gone. both brothers had finished the letter.

"This is good news, Conor," Jack said. "We can set about contacting Brotherhood groups in cities from St. Louis to Chicago. We will arrange the meetings, set up a schedule, then get back to Hobson with the plans. Are one of you planning to bring our response over to Ireland?"

Eamon answered, "No, we can post the response to my brother, Mike. He will see to it that it gets to Hobson. Both Jay and I are planning on staying in America working for Cashman Brothers."

Jack said he understood, then got right back to planning.

"It will take us a fair amount of time to set this all up. I don't even know who to contact in some of these cities," Conor observed.

"Well, Conor, I think the first move is to call a meeting of our members here in Boston. Make a list of all known contacts. I'm sure Dan Foley has a good idea of who to go to in many cities. Then make a trip to New York and go through the same things with them."

It was settled that Conor would call a meeting in Boston within the week. He would follow that up with a trip to New York. They would compile a list of contacts, figure out a travel schedule, then send out the letters to confirm meetings on the dates that fit the schedule. They would shoot for a tour beginning in the spring of 1904. They would attempt to set up meetings in every major city in the east.

Having sorted that all out, the group went back up Derby Street to Tom's house for a family dinner. After dinner, the singing, Irish step dancing from Tom's daughters, and laughter went on into the night. Eamon and Jay felt right at home with their American cousins as they turned in for the night in Jack's guest room.

In the morning, Jack was the first to rise, walking into the kitchen at eight o'clock to find Bridget fixing breakfast.

"How many am I feeding here this morning, Mr. McCarthy, and how many of them will be hungover?" she said with a broad smile.

"Well, there will be five, all hungover, except myself, to answer your question. My question is, why are you so kind as to be here this early taking care of the rabble in this place?"

"It's Saturday morning, and I have nothing else to do than to take care of three drunks and two nice boys who need to see a smiling sober face first thing in the morning."

"It is way too kind of you, Brid, and totally unexpected."

"Sometimes it seems like I'm here all the time."

"Well, maybe you should be here all the time."

The words came out before he even knew what he was saying. They surprised both Jack and Bridget. She turned to look at him, and they held each other's eyes for a long moment before Bridget spoke.

"And what do you mean by that, Mr. McCarthy?"

"I think I mean that perhaps I've been in mourning long enough. I guess I mean my sons need a mother. I guess I mean I would like to be in a courtship with a very kindhearted woman that was once my sister-in-law. That is, of course, if she is of any interest in such a proposal."

Again, a long moment of silence before Bridget said, "Are you sure it's what you want, Jack?"

"We've both been dancing around it for a long time, Brid. I think it's time to address our feelings, assuming you share my feelings." Again silence, so Jack went on, "It would be best if I got an answer before anyone joins us."

"My answer is that I believe you are right. Yes, this kindhearted woman is more than interested."

With that they embraced each other and shared their first kiss. They decided to wait before telling the boys or the rest of the world until they had the chance to get the two families together so they could shock them all at once.

Soon Jack's sons came out for breakfast, joined by the visitors from Ireland. It was hard not to notice a bit more spring in Bridget's step, as well as the looks passed between her and Jack. Still, nothing was said. Eamon and Jay thanked everyone for a great welcome while they headed to the train station with Conor. Next up for them would be meeting with the Cashmans in Boston.

Both Jay and Eamon were very much accustomed to big Irish families. They left big Irish families to come to America. In Salem, they had spent the evening with eight McCarthy relatives. The following night at the large back bay home of James Cashman, they met his family, his brother John's family, and their sister Dierdre's family. Counting Conor, there were seven adult cousins and sixteen Cashman children, six each in James and John's families and four in Dierdre's. It was more than a bit overwhelming. The two spent most of the evening unsuccessfully trying to get the names straight.

Following dinner, which was served to all twenty-five at three different tables, James went over the various jobsites where Cashman Brothers were currently active. It was an impressive list of activities that left both of the boys somewhat in awe of the company started by their uncle, Pat. In the end, James and John decided to start the two off at a project on Boston Harbor where John was overseeing the rebuilding of a commercial pier. They would start work on Monday and were invited to stay at James's home until they put some money together and found living quarters of their own. They retired after the second long night since arriving, feeling more secure about their futures than at any time in their lives. The company they would be working for was large and growing fast. They had a tremendous amount of work on hand with a large crew working steady. They could not have felt any better about their decision to come to America.

CHAPTER XXII

When two people in their forties decide to marry and spend the rest of their days together, it is far different from that same decision being made by two twenty-year-olds. Jack and Bridget were two mature adults who had their eyes wide open as they approached this move. Both had dearly loved Anna Hennessey McCarthy. Both dearly loved John and Bill McCarthy, the children of Anna. They had known each other all their lives, so there was no process necessary for getting used to each other. They had somewhat shocked each other by making the decision. Now it was time to shock everybody else.

On Sunday, Jack told his boys, his brother, Tom, his wife, and his three children that they had all been invited to a brunch after Sunday mass. Bridget told her mother and father that she wanted to treat them to a nice breakfast after mass. She decided to tell her siblings and cousins at a later time.

They all attended Sunday mass at the Immaculate Conception Church. Bridget caught Jack's eye halfway through the service and gave him a wink that he returned. He made sure to lag behind the Hennesseys with his family after mass so as not to have any discussion between the two prior to their arrival at Mike Hennessey's home.

Just as the three Hennesseys were settling into their second-floor home, eight McCarthys were let in the front door by Bridget. Mike turned and asked, "Jack, Tom, what's going on? Is something wrong across the street?"

Tom and Mary and the rest of the group all looked at one another with puzzled expressions. The Hennesseys were, of course, just as puzzled. Then Jack walked over to Bridget, held her hand, and spoke, "We asked everyone here this morning to announce that we have decided to get married and will approach the church today to post the banns next week."

Mike and Pauline Hennessey were at first stunned into silence. John and Bill immediately expressed their outright joy at the idea. John pumped his fist while Bill walked over to hug Bridget. This broke the ice, and everyone else followed suit.

Jack and Bridget had succeeded in delivering a shock to the group, but after that initial reaction, the room was filled with sheer joy. Mike said he could not be happier for the two. Tom expressed the same, and Mary said, "It's about time," to which all laughingly agreed. Bridget and her mother got busy preparing the promised breakfast for all. Mike Hennessey welcomed Jack into his family for the second time. Jack's two boys told him in no uncertain terms that they were thrilled. Everyone felt that a great decision had been made.

Jack and Bridget spent the rest of the day spreading the news to the rest of their families.

Later that week, Conor held his meeting of the Boston chapter of the Fenian Brotherhood with Jack in attendance. It had been one week since receiving the letter from Ireland. Attendance picked up a bit, to thirty-six members, still a far cry from the eighties and nineties, but still an improvement.

He read the letter from Ireland after briefly discussing the initiatives they were looking to fund. The presentation generated a good deal of enthusiasm from the attendees as they saw things moving again. In advance of the meeting, Dan Foley had put together a list of the contacts he was familiar with in major cities. He told the group he was not certain if the list was totally up-to-date, but he had names for New York, Hartford, Cincinnati, Cleveland, Baltimore, Portland, Maine, and Chicago. He was confident other cities could be filled in by the New York group.

Conor had a proposed draft letter that he passed out to the attendees. It called for the brotherhood chapters in various cities to organize gatherings on a date specified in the letter. At the gatherings, the Irish Republican Brotherhood delegation would brief the group on their plans, then explain the need for money to execute their planning. The dates had been arranged so that the traveling group could have time to efficiently move among the various locations.

The meeting ended with a unanimous vote, authorizing Conor and Dan Foley to travel to New York, meet with the leadership of the chapter to verify the list of names Dan provided, and add any names to other cities that they had. The meeting further authorized Conor to send out the letters once the list was complete. Everything Conor had hoped to accomplish in the meeting had worked out perfectly.

Two weeks after the meeting in Boston, Conor and Dan were in New York meeting with that group. New York generated a larger turn-out with well over two hundred in attendance. Conor went through the same exercise of briefing the group on the plans in Ireland. He went into detail on the need for money and explained the plan of having a delegation come over to raise the money. The New York group was in full agreement with the plan. They pledged to do all they could to help. Again, a successful meeting for Conor.

After the meeting, Dan and Conor met with the New York leadership to finalize a list. A number of blanks were filled in, and many on Dan's list confirmed. In the end, the list of cities to be visited included Boston, New York, Portland, Hartford, Philadelphia, Pittsburg, Cincinnati, Cleveland, Chicago, Baltimore, and Kansas City. It was agreed that Conor would draft the response with the schedule of visits. It would be sent to Hobson through Conor's relatives in Cork.

Later in September, the first Baseball World Series was played between the American League team from Boston and the National League team from Pittsburg. At the first game in Boston, Jack made arrangements to meet up with his old friend and baseball player turned boxer, John L. Sullivan. While watching the game, he explained to the champ the tour that had been planned. It was eleven years since he was champ, but he still had star power, especially with the Irish. Jack told him it would be great if he could join them in at least some of the cities.

"I have a pretty tight schedule, Jack, but I applaud what you are doing and will help where I can."

Jack thanked him and left after the game, feeling the wheels were in motion for a fund-raising tour that would fill the coffers of the major players in Ireland. Money from America would be the fuel that powered the engine of the uprising, and Jack, Conor, and the rest of their family would play a major role in raising that money.

CHAPTER XXIII

Hobson, Clark, and McCullough sat around a table in the back room of a safe house in Dublin reviewing the letter from Conor Cashman. The three men were very pleased about where this was going. Money was their greatest need, and America was the greatest source of money. American Irish were not yet far enough removed from their immigration years to have the scars heal. What's more, a good number of Irish, through hard work, had become successful. They tended to be very generous with their funds, especially as it concerned the cause of Irish freedom.

"This is a fantastic opportunity," Hobson began. "The Boston group came over here with two thousand American dollars raised with very little effort. Imagine what we can do traveling to these major cities to tell our story."

"The biggest issue may end up being how we determine where the money goes after we get it," Clark observed. "There are so many competing groups. We need to make sure we control it after we raise it."

"Let's not get ahead of ourselves," Hobson said. "We have yet to raise a nickel. A bit early to worry about where it goes."

"True enough," McCullough chimed in, "but we know our objectives: winning over the Irish people to our cause while we arm and train a military able to fight our oppressors. I think instead of competing organizations a bit of consolidation of organizations around those objectives would be a good idea."

"What do you have in mind?"

"I have not fully thought it all through, but my feeling is that consolidating some of these groups into an organized political party would give us a bully pulpit inside the government to sell our positions."

"You may very well be right, Denis," Hobson noted, "but for now, let's concentrate on raising the money before we start spending it."

With that, the three began writing their answer. They began by informing the Americans that a group called The National Council had been formed to protest the proposed visit of Edward VII. The three drafting the response were active in this effort, as were such dignitaries as W. B. Yeats. They wanted to keep their American allies up-to-date with activities in Ireland, and to emphasize that the Americans were dealing with the right people. The three of them had a hand in just about every rebellious effort. They wanted to make sure the American knew it.

Basically the response agreed with the travel schedule the Americans had proposed. The three travelers from Ireland would plan to arrive in the middle of March. Their efforts would keep them there for an estimated six weeks. However, if they needed more time, they would be prepared to stay longer. They ended with a sincere thank-you and a God blessings to all their American friends. As they wrapped it up, Hobson offered a toast to a successful trip. They all clinked glasses, with broad smiles for one another. This was not only an opportunity to raise the money necessary to achieve their goals, it was also an opportunity to strengthen the hand of these three men. As in all endeavors, there was always competition within the ranks. If they were able to raise the kind of cash they felt was possible, it would strengthen their hand in directing future Republican efforts; certainly a tremendous opportunity for the cause of independence and for the three travelers.

CHAPTER XXIV

In Boston, Conor Cashman and Dan Foley were busy sending out letters to the people they had to contact in the various cities. They had decided to go a step further and visit the places before the March arrival of their three guests in order to stir up enthusiasm in advance of the visit. They wanted to do as much advance work as they could to ensure a successful trip. The two of them went on a seventeen day tour of the targeted cities from St. Louis to Chicago. The Boston chapter of the Fenian Brotherhood agreed to pay the expenses. They not only met with leaders, but where possible, they met the membership of the local organization. Their goal was to build up enthusiasm prior to the arrival of the delegation.

Back in Salem, Jack and Bridget were busy planning a small private wedding ceremony involving only close friends and relatives. There were plenty of McCarthys, Cashmans, and Hennesseys around, so it would be well attended no matter how hard they tried to keep it small. Because of their popularity in the Derby Street neighborhood, they planned a party after the service in McCarthy Brothers store, which would be closed for the day of the wedding. It all went off without a hitch. On October 25, 1904, Bridget Hennessey became Mrs. John McCarthy. Jack's two boys could not have been happier.

Meanwhile a company was proposing to build a coal-fired power plant in the greater Salem area. Several cities in the area were being considered for the location in these very early stages. Many in the Irish neighborhood wanted it located near them for the good-paying jobs it would bring to the area. Jack was able to convince his friend and political mentor, Mike Hurley, to appoint him as the chair of the sighting commission in Salem. This was a very important post because if Salem was chosen as the city to build the facility, the commission would determine where it would go. So in addition to his duties as chair of the finance committee, he now had the additional task of chairing this sighting committee. Add this to his duties at the store as well as his duties as a husband and father, and Jack McCarthy was one busy man. Still his cousin Conor wanted him to attend the meetings in some of the cities, especially when Sullivan would be there.

"I think it would be important for you to be there, Jack. You're an important elected official here in Salem, an Irishman that has succeeded politically. It would help if you were there."

"I will do everything I can to make a few stops with you, Conor, but you need to understand how tight my schedule already is these days."

"I do, Jack, and I will appreciate any time you can give us."

"And what about you, Conor? What of your duties with the family business?"

The two Cashmans from Ireland were responding well to the on-the-job training. They were hard workers who learned fast.

"I tell you, Jack, these two Cashmans that came over from Ireland do the work of two or three men each. They get so much work done, my brothers don't even know I'm not there."

Jack laughed. "It's funny how the arriving immigrants put out so much production that they make us look bad. Next Sunday, I'm going to take Eamon and Jay to Salem for dinner with Tom and me and our families. I have not seen them since the wedding."

"Well, if you have time for dinners, you have time for meetings," Conor said with a wink.

Having agreed to visit some of the cities with Conor, Jack sent him back to Boston with an invitation for Eamon and Jay to take the train up to Salem the following Sunday to have dinner with the McCarthys. They showed up at Jack's door at one o'clock on Sunday. Tom, Mary, and their three children joined them for an early dinner of baked ham with potatoes, carrots, and turnip. The conversation shifted back and forth from family stories from Ireland to tales of their newfound work in construction in America.

"Our cousins really know how to run a construction company," Jay said. "They have more work than they can handle. I've never been so busy."

His brother Eamon nodded his agreement.

Jack said, "Next summer when school's out, you will have a pair of McCarthys on your staff when Tom's son and my son, John, join you. I want you two to teach them how to work as hard as I'm told you two work." This was a comment met with a rolling of the eyes by the two younger McCarthys.

"So you lads are pleased you came over to America? Things have worked out well."

Eamon answered this time, "Yes, things could not be better. We have a great place in Boston, a very exciting city. We have great jobs. I've never had so much extra cash in my life. Still, when Conor goes back to Ireland, we would like to go back for a visit."

"When did Conor say he was going to Ireland? He has not told me anything like that," Jack replied.

"He told us he had some IRB people coming over here, and when they go back, he's planning to go with them."

"Did he say for what purpose?"

"He said he's hoping to bring a number of Irish Americans over to help with the military training. He wants to be one of them," Jay answered.

This was the first Jack had heard of this plan of Conor's. He was a bit disturbed by the news. Raising money to help the cause was one thing, but the thought of his young cousin going over to actively participate in the conflict was a bit unnerving. He decided to tuck it away for now, to be brought up in a later discussion.

The day with Eamon and Jay went well, and the McCarthys were very disappointed it was over, but the two boys had to be at work early on Monday, so they left to catch the train back to Boston at six. They left Jack troubled by the thought of Conor getting so deeply involved in the Irish military. He questioned himself as to his own enthusiasm for the cause and its effects on his younger cousin. If anything happened to Conor, he would surely blame himself for any encouragement he had given him.

CHAPTER XXV

The money tour began in earnest on March 23. The first cities hit were all in New England: Portland, Boston, and Hartford, then on to the Big Apple. The reception in each location was overwhelming. Enthusiastic large crowds listened to Conor Cashman talk about the help that was needed from America as he introduced the three principles from Ireland. They listened to Hobson and McCullough talk about the challenge of gaining the committed support of the great majority of Irish people. They talked about the groups actively seeking to accomplish this objective, as well as the initiatives they were planning, like the newspaper and the formation of a political arm to the movement.

Tom Clark then spoke of the effort to raise, equip, and train a military force capable of standing up to the British Armed Forces. He spoke of the money needed for recruitment as well as for purchasing armaments to equip the force.

He suggested the Irish Americans in the crowd who had served in the military might want to consider a trip over to help with the training or better yet, to join the Irish forces.

After these objectives were all laid out, the three explained the desperate situation of living under John Bull's boot. They spoke of the United States' successful efforts to gain independence and emphasized that independence was just as crucial for Ireland. After all the speeches, they answered questions, and then Conor and his team, including Jack in the New England cities and in New York, would move into the crowd collecting money and pledges from the gathered masses.

As was to be expected, New York brought out the biggest crowds as well as the most money. Donations here included a ten-thousand-dollar donation from successful New York businessman, Donald O'Leary. They also received two twenty-five-hundred-dollar donations from two New York labor unions.

In Boston, both Cashman Brothers Construction and Pat McGowan's real estate company, now being run by his sons, gave five thousand dollars each. Jack and Tom gave two thousand dollars from the store as well as their combined savings.

As they left New York, headed for Baltimore, Jack was headed home to Salem. John L. Sullivan had attended and spoke in New York, intending to do the same in Baltimore. No longer the rock-hard athlete he was when Jack first met him, Sullivan was heavy and bore the signs of a man who drank too much. The years had taken their toll on him. After the New York event, he and Jack and Conor, as well as Dan Foley, all went to an Irish bar to discuss the trip, as well as old times.

"So you went and got married again, Jack, without inviting your old friend Sullivan. I'm crushed."

"It was a very small ceremony, Champ. Nothing like when Anna and I tied the knot."

"Does she look like that beautiful sister of hers that you were lucky enough to marry?"

"There would never be another Anna, but Brid is a very attractive lady, and my two boys love her like a mother."

Conor spoke up, "She's not only a very attractive lady, she has the winning personality of Anna."

"So all and all Jack, life is good for my old friend."

"The second half of the nineties were not good to me, John. But things have bounced back. My boys are growing up right, they're both teenagers now. I'm very busy in Salem government as well as at the store that Tom and I have been running all these years. How about you, John?"

"Well, it's been twelve years since I was the champ, and I have to say they have not all been good ones. I still get a bit of celebrity treatment for my past accomplishments, but I've pissed through a lot of money, Jack. Making it is not as easy as it once was, so I'm not sure where I'm headed."

"Well, celebrity or not, you're always welcome in Salem, Mass, Champ. You're a longtime good friend, the entire neighborhood loves you."

Sullivan put a huge arm around Jack, who was sitting to his right, and gave him a one-arm bear hug.

"Thanks, Jack, you have been a good friend, too. I'm not sure how this strange fellow here," he said, pointing to Conor, "can be related to you, but other than him, you have a great family."

They all laughed at this as Sullivan slapped Conor on the back. As the evening broke up, Jack bid good-bye to all, saying he would catch a train to Boston in the morning, while the others headed to Baltimore. Before retiring for the night, Jack pulled Conor aside to discuss his planned trip to Ireland.

"Conor, I think this is a great thing you're doing, helping these boys raise money. But Jay tells me you are planning to go back with them. What are you thinking?"

"I want to be more active on the ground, Jack, in the front lines, so to speak."

"I was afraid of that. You are stepping into very dangerous territory, Conor. I'm concerned."

"Don't worry, Jack. My eyes are wide open."

Jack let it go at that, but planned to talk again back in Boston.

The tour continued until the last stop in Chicago, which produced a crowd second only to New York. After that stop, they all headed back to Boston, where James and John Cashman put on a welcoming party for all, including the McCarthys from Salem. It was a festive time with plenty of food and drink. It was a successful but exhausting five and a half weeks. They were all glad it was over and all ready to celebrate.

Hobson, McCullough, and Clark could not thank them enough. They weren't even sure yet of the grand total, but it was well over one hundred thousand dollars. It represented the most successful fund-raising effort any group involved in the fight for independence had ever raised. They headed back to Ireland fully prepared to carry on with their objectives and now fully funded as well.

CHAPTER XXVI

Upon returning to Ireland flush with cash, things began to move far more rapidly. Arrangements were quickly made for armament purchases from Germany. The planned Dungannon Clubs were established first in Ulster to promote separation from Britain. This movement gained immediate traction and spread through much of the country. Together with the efforts of the Gaelic Athletic Association, the Gaelic League, and other organizations, the push was on to gain total support from the Irish people. Further initiatives were needed to be taken, and chief among them was the idea around forming a political arm.

The editor of the United Irishman newspaper, Arthur Griffin, had published an article calling for the creation of a political organization joining together a number of groups including his own *cuman na n Gaedheal.* Members of Parliament elected from Ireland had generally supported the idea of it remaining part of the United Kingdom. This was particularly true of Ulster MPs, but generally the case throughout the country. Members of Parliament like John Stewart Parnel would be the exception to this rule. But acting alone, outliers like Parnel had not been able to accomplish any lasting change.

Meanwhile, local authority in Ireland rested with Dublin Castle, the residence of the British Monarch's Irish representative, the Viceroy of Ireland. Members of Parliament in general had little or no control over rulings from "the Castle," as the Viceroy was not answerable to them. This combination left the proponents of independence for Ireland with no government authority in their own country and little voice in the Westminster Parliament.

In an effort to gain a political voice, the Dungannon clubs group, Griffin's *Cumann na n Gaedheal* organization, and the National Council joined together to form the Sinn Fein political party. Sinn Fein meant "we ourselves." This effort attracted the attention of a US citizen, John Devay, who offered funding for a unified party. The voice of independence now had a political presence in the form of this Sinn Fein Party, funded from America.

In another effort to gain popular support, Bulmer Hobson teamed up with Countess Maskievicz to form a youth group. Born Constance Gore-Booth in London in 1868 to a wealthy family, the countess became involved in a number of rebellious activities. Her family owned a large estate in county Sligo, but unlike most land-owners, they treated their tenant farmers well. She married Count Casmir Dunin Markievicz from Poland in 1901, gaining the title of countess. She was involved in the organization of the Irish Citizens Army and many other causes. She remained an active figure in the movement for independence over the years. She was arrested and sentenced to death after the Easter Uprising. The death sentence was later commuted because she was a woman.

Together with Bulmer Hobsen, they organized Na Fianna Ereann, a nationalist youth organization. They emphasized the Irish language, Irish culture, and the need to establish independence for Ireland to the members of this youth organization. Over time, it became a fertile recruiting ground for the Irish Republican Brotherhood.

With the grease of money from America, the wheels were turning faster on the drive for independence. At the same time, events in Europe were taking up the attention of British officials. Their preoccupation with the continent was being keenly followed by Irish leaders, who saw it as forming a window of opportunity for an uprising that may finally succeed. Things were moving fast, with expectations high that something big was coming soon.

CHAPTER XXVII

Back in the United States, Conor continued with his initiative to put together an American force of trained military veterans who could assist in training, as well as fighting when the time was right. During the fund-raising tour, a number of Irish American military veterans had signed up as being interested in going over to Ireland to offer assistance. Conor had written to all fifty-three names that had been on sign-up sheets, but as was to be expected, when it came time to follow through on the commitment, the number had shrunk to under a dozen. Still, Conor was planning a trip in the spring of 1906 with nine other volunteers who were willing to make the voyage. Jack was not a fan of the idea but held off making any comment until the planned trip took shape.

In late summer 1905, with both of his sons working through the summer for Cashman Brothers, Jack and Bridget were at a gathering at James Cashman's house. His son John had heard about the planned trip from his two cousins from Ireland, Eamon and Jay. The two lads were planning to travel along so they could have a visit with their families. John had told his father that the purpose of the trip had something to do with Conor's activities with the Irish militia. He wasn't sure what that meant, but Jack knew exactly what it meant. He took the occasion at James's house to take Conor aside for a chat.

"Conor, you know I have always supported the cause of independence for Ireland. I have supported your efforts and been behind you all the way. I'm proud of how you have revived the Fenian Brotherhood in Boston. But I'm very concerned with where you are taking matters now. Financial support is one thing, but physically joining the battle, that's a whole other deal, and a very dangerous one."

Conor had been expecting pushback from his brothers, as well as Jack. "I know what I'm getting into, Jack. It's the passion of my life. You and my brothers are happy with your business, with your families. I'm not made that way, I crave adventure. I crave justice for a land that's been burdened too long. I have to do this."

"So your intention even goes beyond training, you would actually join the armed battle."

"I would, Jack."

There was an extended silence as the two cousins held eye contact. Jack broke the silence. "Conor, you're a grown man who has to make his own decisions. Like the rest of us, you have to do whatever is necessary for you to live with yourself. God be with you and keep you safe." With that, he embraced his younger cousin. Jack determined that he would never bring the matter up again.

Later, Jack had an opportunity to talk with Eamon about the brothers' trip back home.

"We plan to stay two weeks. That should give us time to see everyone and tell them all how great we have it here," Eamon explained.

"Do you think you will be bringing more Cashmans back here with you, Eamon?"

Eamon smiled at this, saying, "It's a possibility, Jack. We are very happy working here."

While Conor's activities had not escaped Jack's attention, they had also caught the attention of the special unit in the British Embassy assigned to monitor the Fenian Brotherhood activity. Early one morning, two men entered the office of Cashman Brothers construction, catching Jay before he left for the jobsite. They announced themselves as Mr. Myers and Mr. Harris from the British Embassy, asking if they could have a few moments of Jay's time.

"I'm very busy, gentlemen, so only a few minutes. Come into the back office."

Jay led them into the office he shared with his brother, telling them to take a seat. "What can I do for you, gentlemen?"

"Well, Mr. Cashman, you run a very successful company here in Boston," Myers began. "We have watched the growth over the past decade, it is truly remarkable."

"Thank you, but you two didn't come here to compliment my company, and I don't have a lot of time, so get to the point." Jay was not always so blunt, but he had taken somewhat of an instant dislike for these two.

"Okay, then, we work for a special unit in the embassy that monitors the activities of the Fenian Brotherhood." Myers waited for but did not receive a response.

"We have taken particular interest in the activities of your brother, Conor." Again, he waited but did not receive a response.

"Are you aware of your brother's activities?"

"What my brother does is his business, I'm not his keeper."

"True enough. But we know you have contributed money to some of his efforts." Again, he waited but did not receive a response.

"I have to say, Mr. Cashman, that these activities, if they persist, could very well have a damaging effect on the continued success of your business."

"Are you threatening me, you little weasel?" Now Jay waited for a response and didn't get one, so he rose from his seat and walked around his desk, pointed at the two, and said, "You both have exactly ten seconds to get up and out of here, or I will personally start a shoe factory up your asses."

"Now, Mr. Cashman—"

"Get the fuck out of my office. Nine, eight, seven—" he began the countdown. The two Brits got up and hurried out the door.

Later that day, as Jay joined up with his brothers, they all shared a hearty laugh about the incident. When the laughter was over, Jay said to his younger brother, "Conor, I do not worry about those two arseholes causing any trouble for our company. Their British bullshit is about as welcome in Boston as the plague. But you watch your back, little brother, especially while you are in Ireland. You know we will always have your back, but when you're over there, you're on your own. Be careful."

Conor assured his brother that he knew what he was getting into. He would be sure to exercise caution at all times and return safely back to Boston. His brothers appreciated the assurances, but their fears were not alleviated.

CHAPTER XXVIII

Over the next several years, Conor would make several trips to Ireland with groups of Irish Americans who had served in the military. As predicted, it was a lot to ask for men to take time away from family and work to travel across the ocean for the cause of Irish freedom. His first group included nine members besides himself. That figure decreased every trip, until his fourth and final trip, which included only two military veterans. He did, however, enjoy the company of two kindred spirits, Kevin Conley of Portland and David O'Neil of Chicago, on all four of his excursions. These two gentlemen were as dedicated to the cause as Conor himself. Like Conor, they were ready not only to help train, but also to join in the fighting if and when it broke out.

Before the trip, Conor made it a point to gather together as much money from the various chapters of *Clanna n Gael* as he could so he could bring that over with him. While in Ireland, Conor's group would spend time speaking to groups within the IRB about military strategy, as well as training. They lectured about the need for discipline within the ranks, the value of a solid chain of command, and above all, the cardinal rule that soldiers must follow orders. They would participate in training exercises, but only as instructors. The Irish volunteers appreciated their participation. They were respected as voices of experience who had served in the US military rather than the British forces. Up until their arrival, the only experienced support came from veterans of the British military who were not afforded the same respect because of the military organization they had served.

Conor initially dealt with Hobson, McCullough, and Clark, the three travelers to the US who were all members of the supreme council of the IRB. As time went on, he met other major players, like Sean MacDiamada, Patrick Pearce, Jim Larkin, and James Connolly. He had rapidly become as welcome and trusted a member of the movement as any native son by those in the inner circle.

Conor had asked his cousin Jack to join him on all his training trips, but Jack had answered that he had to tend to business at home. Much had happened with him over the same period. Jack settled very quickly into a very close and comfortable relationship with his new wife. He would have never thought it possible for him to ever feel at home again in a marriage to anyone after Anna. He was wrong, as the marriage to Bridget proved to be as great a relationship between two people as his first marriage had been. They shared life together, taking care of the boys, working at the store, and spending their free time together.

Through his political influence, he had been able to move both his sons into postal employment right after they graduated from high school. This provided them with solid, secure, and good-paying jobs. He had also managed to secure the location of the proposed coal-fired power plant to the north end of Derby Street. Construction began in the fall of 1909 with all the accompanying employment. The jobs being filled by a good few residents of the Irish neighborhood only helped enhance his popularity. The store continued to prosper, so as Jack approached his fifties, he was wrapping up his public service while concentrating more on the store and his family. In line with that, he did agree to join his cousin on the fourth and final training trip. Bridgett Hennessey had never had a trip to Ireland, so Jack thought it would be a good time for her to see the homeland and visit her relatives in Kilkenny. John and Bill could help cover time at the store in between their work at the post office, and as always, Tom was supportive. Bridget was excited about the trip and anxious to meet her relatives.

They headed over in early April 1910. Jack had suggested his brother Tom and Mary should join them, but Tom was far happier working in Salem than he would be traveling, so it was Jack, Bridget, Conor, Kevin Conley, and David O'Neil. As they landed at Cobh Harbor, Jack agreed to sit in with Conor's group as they met with

Tom Clark. After that, Jack and Bridget would head to Kilkenny, while Conor's group would head off to take care of business.

The meeting took place in Jack's hotel room rather than a public place. The four Americans were crammed in with Clark, while an associate of Clark waited in the lobby. Jack had met him on his trip to the US, and of course, Conor had been dealing with him for years. After initial greetings, Clark welcomed them all home, then got right into business. He was a very serious operator who had little room for small talk. He had spent years on the inside the anti-British efforts, had served time in a British prison, and had become very hardened by it all.

"There is a confluence of events happening here that will bring things to a head soon. It's simply a matter of picking the right time."

"You make it sound like it's a powder keg ready to blow," Conor observed.

"That it is, lad, that it is. The only question is when will it blow."

"When it does, Kevin, David and I want to be right here with you, joining the fight."

Jack let this comment go by, but it served to rekindle his concerns about his cousin's commitment.

"We will need all the help we can get, Conor. As you Yanks know, escaping from under John Bull's boat is not an easy task." With that, Clark went into the details on where he had scheduled Conor and company to spend their time meeting with volunteer forces. He wanted to keep the three of them together and move them around to several locations. Jack only half listened while he waited for the session to end so he could grab a moment with Conor. That opportunity came a bit more than an hour later as Clark was shaking hands to leave. Jack pulled Conor aside.

"Conor, we have had this discussion before, but I have to say again that you are committing yourself to grave danger with this idea that you would be here to join in the fighting. I know how strongly you feel about it. but for God's sake, think about what you are committing yourself to do."

His plea to his cousin was more emotional than past discussions. There was a storm brewing, and the danger of Conor's intending to pick up arms in the fight was far more immediate.

Conor placed his hand on Jack's shoulder, looked him in the eye, and spoke. "I have, Jack. Give me the respect to know that I'm not stupid. I know how I feel, I know what's important to me. I know what my commitment is." Conor stared into his cousin's eyes. Jack could not help but be impressed by his cousin's commitment and his sincerity.

As at the end of their last discussion on this matter, Jack embraced his younger cousin, vowing to respect his decision. Still he remained concerned for his cousin. He did not mention it to Bridget but spent a restless night thinking of where it would end. The next morning, Conor headed for his first assignment while Jack and Bridget headed for Kilkenny.

It had been twenty-three years since Jack had visited the Hennesseys in Kilkenny. On that trip, he and Anna had attended a reception at the farm of her uncle, Colon, attended by ten aunts and uncles and seventeen cousins. Colon had since passed away, so the farm was now owned by his son Martin, who had been a seventeen-year-old spitfire on Jack's first visit. He proved to be just as grand of a host as his father had been, welcoming his cousin Bridget, while renewing his acquaintances with Jack. Bridget was six when her family left for America. She had a vague memory of Colon, but so much time had passed, it was hard for her to picture him.

The couple stayed at the farm for three days. Instead of one huge gathering as was the case on Jack's first visit, they were treated to a new wave of cousins every day, who traveled different distances to meet the Americans. At the end, Bridget had met even more cousins than Anna, while experiencing the same problem of trying to remember the names. She was welcomed home by all, and she never felt any more like part of a family than they all made her feel. Jack was also welcomed home and made to feel part of the family. They invited all those cousins they met to come over to America for a visit, but noticed a lack of enthusiasm for the idea.

From Kilkenny, they went back to the Cork area to spend some time with Cashman relatives of Jack. Just as in Kilkenny, the two Cashmans who organized the reception in 1887, Sean and Grainne, had passed away. They spent time with Sean Jr., who took them on a guided tour to many of the other Cashmans in the area. Again there was no grand gathering of the clan, just a number of meetings at various locations. It wasn't the grand tour of twenty-three years ago, but it was an enjoyable visit with a number of relatives who had grown increasingly distant. Just as in Kilkenny, both Jack and Bridget were made to feel like family. Sean Jr. was a very successful farmer and was also active in the Irish Republican Brotherhood.

Following the stop in Cork, they went on to Killarney. This portion of the trip was for pure sightseeing. They took in the beauty of the Lakes of Killarney, took a jaunty cart ride through the Gap of Dunlow. They spent time on the Ring of Kerry as well as the Dingle Peninsula, where they climbed up to Conor Pass. After a full three weeks of taking in the beauty of Ireland, they headed back to Cobh Harbor for the return trip. Bridget had fallen in love with the country and the Irish people. She was sorry it had taken her so long to come back to her birth place.

"You grow up in an Irish family hearing the stories about how beautiful the country is, but until you see it for yourself, it's impossible to imagine."

"So you enjoyed the sights, did you?"

"Jack, the Lakes of Killarney, the coast of Kerry, the Ring, the Cork and Kerry Mountains, it's all so breathtaking, it's a shame any of us ever had to leave."

The millions of Irish forced to leave their country by the great hunger and by British abuse was a very dark spot in the history of a great country.

Jack was in total agreement with that statement. They boarded the ship for home with him thinking it would be his last trip to Ireland. He was not taking into account the future plans of his cousin, Conor.

CHAPTER XXIX

Conor Cashman, Kevin Conley, and David O'Neil stayed in Ireland for eight months. There was a sense among all three that something could break at any time, so they were reluctant to leave. Finally, in April 1911, they boarded a ship for the return trip, vowing to return as soon as things came to a head. Meanwhile they would keep a sharp eye from their perch in America as events unfolded in Ireland.

Over the next few years, events did indeed unfold as things were moving at an ever-accelerated pace. There was a renewed push for a Home Rule Bill in the Westminster Parliament. Prime Minister Asquith introduced this third attempt, and it prompted a strong reaction in Ireland's northeasternmost six counties. Sir Edward Carson and James Craig set up the Ulster Volunteer Force (UVF) to defend Ulster against home rule. In reaction to this, the Irish Volunteer Force (IVF) was established within the IRB to "secure the rights and liberties common to all the people of Ireland." This force grew rapidly with upward of one hundred thousand members by 1914, which was a positive sign that the efforts to win the hearts and minds of the Irish people for the cause of independence was working.

Meanwhile, the labor movement in Ireland was creating its own force. Jim Larkin had founded the Irish Transportation and General Workers Union. In August of 1913, a giant union rally was attacked by the Dublin Metropolitan police, killing two of the union strikers. This was hardly the first incidence of brutality against union members during strikes or rallies. So Larkin, together with James Conley, established the Irish Citizens Army to protect striking workers. It seemed like every day, a new report would reach Conor describing the unrest in Ireland. He either found it in newspaper articles or letters he received from his cousins. The biggest story out of Europe, of course, was the ongoing threat of war. It became more likely each day that a major European conflict was only months away. A war in Europe would create the distraction that would require the British to focus their attention someplace other than Ireland.

In March of 1914, Conor showed up in Salem to meet with his cousin, Jack. He had made his decision that it was time for him to go back to Ireland and to join the fray. He had discussed the matter with his two closest allies in this cause, Kevin Conley and David O'Neil. Conley was ready to go with him; O'Neil could not leave for several months, but would join them later. As always, Conor sought the council of his cousin before making final arrangements. He had cleared things with his two older brothers, so Jack was the last hurdle.

They sat together in Jack's kitchen after he had closed the store. Bridget was fixing dinner while listening in on the discussion. Like Jack, Bridget was concerned for Conor's safety as he headed back to a troubled land.

"I know you think it's too dangerous for me to be over there joining in the fighting. We've talked about it before, and my brothers feel the same as you. But you all need to understand that I need to do this."

"Conor, it troubles me deeply because I can't help but feel that my own involvement in the Fenian Brotherhood had an influence on you that has led to this stage where you are willing to risk your life." This was the first time Jack had explained to Conor that he harbored guilty feelings concerning Conor's commitment to the danger of joining the fight.

"You weren't alone, Jack. My own father was as active as you in the Brotherhood. He contributed a great deal of money, as have my brothers."

"All true, Conor, because we all have the same desire to see the country of our fathers free from the British. But that's the point, it's the country of our fathers. We are Americans now. We were born and raised Americans. Is it still our fight over there to the extent that we take up arms?"

"We differ on this, Jack. I feel that it is my fight for my father and all the Cashmans before him, for the McCarthys who starved to death and were buried in a common grave, for centuries of ridicule and abuse from a ruling class only interested in their own wealth, for the stigma that the British placed on our people that followed them here so that they were ridiculed and abused when they arrived, for the suffering, and to rid the country of a harsh, uncaring people who sat idly by and watched children starve to death, for all that, it's still my fight." Conor's voice raised with each line he spoke, and he pounded his fist on the table at the end.

Jack had no response to this reasoning that was delivered with such emotion that it brought tears to his eyes.

In the silence that followed, Bridget walked over and hugged Conor with tears in her eyes, and she said, "We love you, Conor, and Jack and I are both proud of you."

The discussion of the subject was over except for Jack and Bridget giving Conor their support. They had dinner then joined with Tom, Mary, and the younger McCarthys for an evening of good cheer. Conor left in the morning, with Jack unsure if he would ever see him again.

On June 30, Conor and Kevin Conley boarded a ship for Ireland. They met with Tom Clark and Bulmer Hobson upon their arrival. At the meeting, they were told of rifle and ammunition shipments from Germany. They learned of the training and of the Irish Volunteer Force. They were very encouraged to hear of the size of this force. Also encouraging was the news of the gun shipments. They left the meeting with the strong feeling that the forces were aligned. They were sure that the rebellion would begin soon, and the pieces were in place for it to be a success.

Shortly after their arrival, two things happened that resulted in a final push toward an uprising. First, on August 4, war was declared in Europe. The First World War had begun. The Home Rule Bill that had passed parliament was delayed by Britain until the end of the war. Meanwhile, Irish rebel forces were emboldened by the fact that British forces would be occupied by the war and unable to react as strong to an uprising. The hoped-for distraction was upon them.

The second thing that happened was the joining together of the Irish Volunteer Force and the Irish Citizens Army. This not only brought the two forces together, it resulted in James Connolly being placed on the newly formed military council with the IRB. This seven-man council began the planning for the Easter Uprising. As all this unfolded, Conor and Kevin Conley were in the middle of it all.

The two Americans were being used in a number of different capacities, including helping to unload a second gun shipment from Germany and then distributing the guns and ammo to different locations. They participated in some training exercises. They got involved in the internal struggle in the IRB with some members advocating the involvement of Irish trained forces joining the British armed forces to fight in WWI. Conor and Kevin helped discourage that idea among the units with which they worked. The cause of the Irish independence was far more important than helping the Brits fight the Germans. After all, Germany had been the number-one supplier of armaments to Irish rebels.

In December of 1915, Conor and Kevin were called into a meeting in Dublin with Tom Clark and Thomas MacDonaugh, two of the seven members on the military council. Both Conor and Kevin were aware that the council was planning something big, but their activities were kept very secretive. Conor believed that what they were planning would be happening soon. This meeting confirmed his belief.

In attendance, along with the two military council members, was Eamon McAleney, an officer in the IVF. Clark spelled out the mission for the two Americans.

"We have had another shipment of arms from Germany seized by the British. We remain short on arms and ammunition. The constabulary keeps heavy stashes of arms in several locations around the country. One of these locations is Kilkenny. Our aim is to attack several of these locations, take the arms, and destroy the barracks. The arms you capture will be needed very shortly so this is a key mission. Eamon will lead a raid on the Royal Constabulary in Kilkenny and we need you two to be part of his force."

"We are ready for action," Conor replied as Kevin nodded his agreement. "When will the raid take place?"

"You have all the information you need for now. We need you to report for duty in two months, February 25 at Sean Kelley's farm outside Kilkenny. Eamon will give you directions. You will be met there by the rest of the raiding force."

With that, the two Americans were dismissed. They left excited by the idea that they would be seeing action for the first time. They went to Cork to spend the holidays with Sean Cashman and the rest of Conor's relatives. On orders from their superiors, they did not mention the upcoming raid. The first two months of 1916 were excruciating as they waited out the days until they reported for duty. Finally, the big day came, and they reported to Sean Kelley's farm.

Over the next two weeks, they went over the plan of attack on the barracks. They would strike early under cover of darkness. An incendiary device would be thrown through a back window at the same time the front door would be smashed in by four men carrying a battering ram. These four would be followed in by six additional volunteers, the constables either killed or captured, the weapons seized, and the barracks destroyed. The attack force went through more than half a dozen trial runs of the plan of attack to make sure they all knew their roles.

At 4:30 a.m. on the morning of March 12, 1916, fourteen men attacked as planned. Their advance observations told them there were eight constables on duty. It was wartime, and the barracks that housed large supplies of weapons were manned twenty-four hours a day. Conor had volunteered to be one of the four men carrying the battering ram. As such, he was among the first to enter the barracks. The constable behind the desk reacted fast, and shot Sean Kelley square in the chest. He was dead when he hit the floor. The remaining three volunteers in the first wave had now readied their rifles as a second constable came through the door leading to the back room. He fired a shot at Cashman that missed wide. As he aimed for a second shot, Cashman aimed his own rifle at his assailant. They fired at each other simultaneously. Cashman's bullet struck home, hitting the constable in the chest, killing him. Conor had no time to digest this as the bullet from the constable tore through his shoulder, knocking the rifle from his grasp while knocking him down.

Fighting went on for another fifteen minutes all around a wounded Conor Cashman. In the end, six constables were killed and two were wounded. Four volunteers were killed and four more wounded, including Cashman. The armaments were taken while the incendiary device thrown through the window did its work burning the barracks to the ground. The weapons and wounded were carted off to a safe house. Mission accomplished.

CHAPTER XXX

With all the years of planning, training, and preparation, the military forces of the Irish nationals lacked a number of essentials for a military force. Communications were poor, trained leadership was lacking, and perhaps most of all, they lacked medical care for the wounded. Conor was bleeding badly from a wound that needed a proper field dressing, the capabilities of which were not available. The other men did their best to stop the bleeding, but there was no one in the group with medical training. Kevin Conley tried valiantly to help his friend, but he too lacked any training.

The four wounded volunteers were taken to a safe house outside of Kilkenny. The first trained medical attention came from a nurse and a midwife who were both supportive of the movement. One of the wounded had been shot in the chest, so there was really no hope for survival. Two of the others only suffered superficial wounds, so they could be put back together quite easily. Conor, on the other hand, was a different matter. The bullet had hit him low in the left shoulder just above and to the left of his heart. He had already lost a good deal of blood by the time they got to him. They were able to stop the bleeding, but he was very weak, and the bullet needed to come out. A hospital stay was not an option. He would be detained by the British and tried for treason. He needed a doctor as well as a long period of rest to recover.

Thankfully, there were doctors who also supported the cause. They were able to get one to Conor on the following day. At this point, he was barely alive and in dire need of a blood transfusion. The doctor was concerned that the loss of blood would cause Conor to go into shock. In addition he was afraid he would not survive the ordeal of removing the bullet, but it had to come out. He first set up a transfusion using a nurse as the donor. This was a relatively new medical procedure made more difficult by virtue of not being in a hospital. He performed the surgery necessary to remove the bullet even as the transfusion was taking place. There were no blood banks, and he had no means to test for blood types, but it was essential that at least a pint of blood be added to Conor's system; thankfully, the donor's blood was compatible.

After removing the bullet, he dressed the wound. He prescribed complete rest for an extended period. It was dangerous for both Conor, as well as the owners of the safe house, for him to be there. The doctor said he could not be moved for at least two or three weeks. His friend Kevin said he would stay to guard the house until they could move him to cousin's home outside of Cork. Kevin made sure his friend got the rest and nourishment he needed. Daily visits from the nurse, and doctor visits whenever possible, kept him improving day after day.

Seventeen days later, as Conor began to show signs of his strength returning, the IRB provided a wagon to transfer him to Sean Cashman's farm outside of Cork. Kevin stayed with him the entire time until he was safe.

Back in America, Conor's brothers were made aware by a letter from Sean Cashman that Conor had been wounded. They notified Jack, who immediately took the train into Boston to meet with his cousins. They discussed their options, but because of the war, which was being waged at sea as well as land, their options were few. Travel was restricted as well as dangerous, given the state of affairs in Europe. David O'Neil had found this to be true when he had attempted to get to Ireland to join Conor and Kevin. He never made it there. Jack and his cousins were running into the same issue. What further complicated things was the fact that they could not involve the State Department because Conor was wounded fighting against a US ally, Great Britain, in a time of war. Any involvement by State Department officials would undoubtedly result in Conor's arrest by the British government. Treason was punishable by death.

If the three of them were able to somehow get themselves smuggled into Ireland, they would never be able to sneak Conor out. So the whole situation resulted in the people on the American side of the ocean worrying through forced inactivity and receiving periodic updates from their relatives while waiting out World War I.

In Ireland, Conor was settling into an extended rehabilitation. He was extremely restless because he knew things were about to happen. He was not sure exactly what was planned, but he knew something big was about to break. Being wounded and enduring a long period of rehabilitation was not what Conor had in mind when he returned to Ireland. He wanted to be in on the action. He expressed his frustration daily to his friend, Kevin, who stayed by his side the entire time. What he was about to miss would become known as the Easter Uprising. It would be seen historically as the beginning of the Irish War of Independence.

CHAPTER XXXI

Kevin Conley stood by Conor's side as he rehabbed in his cousin's farmhouse. Many Cashman relatives stopped by to see him, but his presence needed to be kept secret for fear the constabulary would find out his whereabouts and arrest him. Conley was there to guard the house, as well as his friend.

On April 18, a member of the raiding group on the Kilkenny barracks, Jack O'Brian, came to the farmhouse to talk with Kevin. They met outside, having a long conversation while they walked around the grounds. At the end of their talk, Kevin told him he would have to go in and talk with Conor before he could leave. He walked into his friend's room to find Conor sitting in a chair, looking out the window. Still very weak, he was not unaware of what was going on around him.

"So can I assume Jack is here to take you on another mission?"

"You're very observant, my friend."

"I want to go along, Kevin. I can ride in the back of a cart until we get where we are going. By the time we get there, I'll be ready for action."

"This is not going to be over in a day or a week, Conor. We are in it for the long haul. Stay here until you're fully recovered. There will be other battles."

Conor looked at his friend and finally nodded his head in agreement. "Okay, Kevin, but you keep your head down and your wits about you. Don't be running into a bullet like your dumbass friend."

With that, they embraced one another as Kevin took his leave. He did not tell Conor where he was going. Conor, knowing the value of keeping things secret, didn't ask. Kevin was headed to Dublin.

He had not yet been fully briefed, but he knew it was for something big. His briefing came from Jack O'Brian on the journey to Dublin. Conor sat in his chair as his friend left, reflecting on his situation. His wound and recovery had resulted in his missing what he knew was a major event in the struggle. He could not have felt any more depressed.

The seven-member military council had planned the Easter Uprising. The British were at war, and troop levels in Ireland were low. What's more, the Germans would help, so the timing seemed right. A shipment of guns was due to arrive in Tralee Bay several days before Easter. The IVF would be armed properly and ready to fight. The main attack would be in Dublin. There would be others against constabulary barracks in Galway, Cork, and other areas, but the main thrust would be to secure key locations in Dublin. Once that was done, they would declare the free Irish state.

They anticipated the British would then try to send in reinforcements. It would be difficult for them to commit too many forces because of their battles with Germany. So the plan was to station IVF forces along the main routes into Dublin to slow down, or even stop, the advance of the reinforcements. Kevin would be stationed along one of the routes.

The planned uprising took place on the day after Easter as several events delayed it by one day.

As is usually the case, the best-laid plans don't always run smoothly. Things got off to a bad start when the German gun shipment was intercepted by the British. This caused the uprising to be delayed. It also caused confusion when the head of the IVF, Eoin MacNeil, sent out a counter-manding order. Still, on April 24, some twelve hundred IVF and citizens army members took over the Dublin General Post Office, the four courts, Jacob's Factory, Boland's Mill, the South Dublin Union, St. Stevens Green, and the College of Surgeons. They made the General Post Office their headquarters with five members of the military council stationed there. They removed the British flag, replacing it with the Irish flag, while Patrick Pearce stood on the steps and read the proclamation of the Irish Republic proclaiming Irish independence. The challenges now would be to defend their positions, thereby defending their independence.

The British had been caught unprepared, now it was up to those stationed on the roadways leading to Dublin to slow any advance by reinforcements. Kevin Conley, armed and ready, waited along with just under one hundred volunteers for the arrival of British troops.

The planned raids in other areas, like Galway, Wexford, and Cork, were less successful. The seized German gun shipment left these areas short of arms, while the confused communications early on only made matters worse. For both sides in the conflict, Dublin was the focus.

News of the uprising spread fast. Sean Cashman came into Conor's room Tuesday morning with the news that Dublin was in the hands of the Irish nationalists. Conor was ecstatic, even if somewhat disappointed that he was not there.

"God, this is great, Sean. I only wish I were there."

"Well, it is a great step forward, but it's far from over. The British will not take this lying down. They will fight back."

"They will surely want to, but they have their hands full with other issues all over Europe. They're spread too thin to react with the necessary force."

Conor was very optimistic, but his cousin was realistic. "Don't underestimate them, Conor. We have made that mistake too many times."

Over the next six days, the British proved Sean to be absolutely right. The British sent in over sixteen thousand troops. Fighting along the roads going into Dublin was fierce. Kevin Conley's position was one of the first hit as thousands of British troops overwhelmed the roughly 140 volunteers. The initial gun battle was so intense that a good number of the volunteer force deserted. Those that stayed, including Kevin, faced not only overwhelming numbers, but the power of the British artillery that made their rifles seem as overmatched as the numbers. In the end, twenty-six volunteers were either dead or wounded, another two dozen had deserted, and the remaining were captured. The captured included Kevin Conley, who had also taken a bullet in the leg. Other positions established to intercept reinforcements did not fare any better. British firepower was simply too much for the IVF forces.

In the city, the British troops were supported by heavy artillery and a naval gunboat. Positions being held by the IVF forcers were surrounded and pounded with artillery and machine gun fire. The heavy-handed British response resulted in a huge number of civilian casualties. In all, 485 were killed and 2600 wounded. Over 50 percent of them were civilians, many of whom had nothing to do with the uprising. The powerful response was not expected, given the war the British were engaged in on the continent. The loss of innocent lives, as well as destruction of Dublin buildings, was devastating.

In order to avoid more civilian casualties, Patrick Pearce surrendered unconditionally on April 29 to Brigadier General Lowe who had led the British troops. News of the surrender also traveled fast. Back in County Cork, Conor Cashman took the news very hard. Given his own slow healing wounds, and his lack of knowledge about what happened to Kevin Conley, all adding to the news of surrender, threw him into a depression. Still, even in this depressed state, his resolve to see this through to a positive end remained strong. He had made up his mind he would not leave Ireland until it was a free country.

The aftermath of the Easter Uprising was severe, and it shaped the future far more than the British anticipated. Because of the many civilian casualties, the initial reaction of the Irish people was not favorable to the rebels. This initial reaction was made more unfavorable for the rebels by the fact that Irish families had relatives fighting as part of the British armed forces in the war in Europe. This antirebel sentiment would be quickly turned around by the harsh reaction from the British toward the rebel forces.

In order to set an example to discourage any action of this type in the future, the British commenced trials of treason immediately. Over a five-day period in early May, fourteen rebels were convicted of treason and executed. This included the seven-man military council's Patrick Pearce, Thomas MacDonagh, Thomas Clark, Joseph Plunkett, Eamon Ceannt, James Connolly, and Sean MacDianada, as well as William Pearse, Edward Daly, Michael O'Harahan, John

MacBride, Michael Mallin, Sean Henston, and Conor Colbert. They even sentenced the Countess Maskievics to death, but her sentence was commuted because she was a woman.

In addition to the executions, 3,500 people were taken prisoners under martial law. Many of these prisoners ended up in British prisons. Included in this group of prisoners was Kevin Conley. He would spend the next two years in prison. In late 1917 and early 1918, the Parliament in Westminster was attempting another vote on home rule. The idea was that a positive vote on home rule would help end the push for independence. In an effort to gain support from Irish people, the prisoners taken after the Easter Rebellion were released, including Kevin Conley.

The execution and arrests outraged Irish public opinion, turning it from being hostile to the rising to a wave of nationalism and anti-British hostility. It would result in the overwhelming support of the pro-independence political party, Sinn Fein. In the 1918 elections, Sinn Fein won 73 of Ireland's 105 seats to the British Parliament.

In January 1919, these seventy-three elected officials refused to take their seats in Westminster. Instead they declared the independence of the Irish Republic and established their own seat of government in Dublin. In establishing their own seat of government, they again declared an Irish state just as they had on the day of the Easter Uprising. This time, they made the claim on a foundation of political support. They were accomplishing by an electoral mandate what they had failed to accomplish by military force. However, just like after the Easter Uprising, military force would be necessary to maintain the independence they declared. Thus began the Irish War of Independence.

Chapter XXXII

Back in Massachusetts, both the Cashmans in Boston and the McCarthys in Salem kept up-to-date on Conor's condition through correspondence from their cousins in Cork. They were still unable to get to Ireland to try to bring him home as World War I raged on. They agreed that as soon as the war ended, they would head over to bring Conor home. Both of his brothers, as well as Jack, regretted not being able to talk Conor out of his mission to take up arms against the British.

In the meantime, Cashman Brothers Construction continued to grow and prosper, as did Jack McCarthy's store in Salem. Jack had purchased land on Loring Avenue in a more upscale neighborhood than Derby Street. He intended at some point to sell the store and move the entire family to Loring Avenue. His oldest son, John, had married and was sharing the apartment over the store with his wife, Clara, and two children, Joseph and Anna. His son, Bill, was spending a lot of time with a young lady, so he too would be marrying at some point. So Jack was running out of room on Derby Street.

On February 2, 1918, Jack's longtime friend, John L. Sullivan, died. His last five or six years had not been good, as the old fighter did not age well. Jack joined Sullivan's old opponent, Jake Kilrain, as a pallbearer at the large Boston funeral for that city's first sports hero. It was twenty-six years since he was the champ, but his popularity in Boston remained very high. Jack mourned the loss of a longtime good friend. He sat during the funeral reminiscing about that night many years ago, in O'Shea's pub, when they first met, and their trip to Ireland while he was Champion of the World. Sullivan was a man who gave hope and pride to the downtrodden Irish people. Sullivan had been all that, but most importantly, he had been Jack's good friend. They had a friendship that lasted almost forty years. Even though they had many of those years when they saw each other infrequently, Jack would still miss him.

On November 11, 1918, the first World War ended. One week later, Jack McCarthy and James Cashman made arrangements to travel to Ireland to see Conor. Getting him out of the country would still be a challenge as he remained a wanted man. Still, the two travelers felt it was time for Conor to come home, so they were up to the challenge. The biggest problem they were going to encounter would not be the British, it would be Conor himself.

They landed in Cobh Harbor on December 16 and went right to Sean Cashman's farm outside Cork City in Killy Donohue. Conor had long since recovered and moved out of Sean's. He was again active in the aftermath of the Easter Uprising. He remained a member of the Irish Volunteer Force, as well as the Irish Republican Brotherhood. In spite of the setback loss in the Easter Uprising, the rebel groups were riding high on the wave of public support. Sinn Fein had won the great electoral victory, and all signs pointed to a renewed effort at independence.

Sean greeted the travelers, welcoming them home. "I know you are anxious to see Conor. He is aware of your arrival date, so he should be here any day. He has been very active. I haven't laid eyes on him for months, but I did get word to him so he should be here anytime."

The travelers were obviously disappointed to have missed Conor, but they were glad to see their cousin, Sean.

"Sean, we really appreciate you helping Conor recover from his wounds, as well as you hiding him out to keep from arrest. We will never forget it."

"Well, Jim, maybe we will send a couple more Cashmans over to join the two you've taken such good care of these past years."

"Glad to take more Cashmans. They're my best workers. Eamon and Jay have both made a great life for themselves in Boston. The more Cashmans in Boston, the better off the city will be."

"Where is Conor's head these days?" Jack asked. "Is he ready to come home?"

"Not by a long shot. He is more committed than ever, Jack. I will let him speak for himself, but if your intention is to pack him up to take home, you may have wasted your time."

The two stayed overnight at Sean's, dining and talking with a number of other relatives. The next morning, they awoke to find Conor sitting at the kitchen table. They embraced each other, then sat down with cups of tea and full Irish breakfasts. The initial conversation was all about Conor getting filled in on what was going on in Boston and Salem with his relatives. When breakfast was finished, James broke the ice to discuss the major issue of Conor's return home.

"Conor, you've performed here far beyond the call of duty. You've been wounded, almost died. Don't you think it's time to come home?"

"Not even close, brother. The work is not done. We are still not independent."

"Conor, this battle could go on for years," Jack said. "You know I want to see an independent Ireland as much as you do, but for God's sake, you can't do it on your own."

"With respect, Jack, you may want an independent Ireland, but you don't want it as bad as I do. You couldn't. I live and breathe it constantly. I want it so bad I can taste it."

"Okay, Conor, I will give you that. But this could drag on for years and years."

"Good things are going on that I can't talk about. But you saw the great electoral victory that Sinn Fein just pulled off. That changes everything. We have the political clout now to take legal action to achieve independence."

"The British won't settle for that, Conor. They are not going to give in just because a rogue group of political figures take some action. You saw that with the Easter Uprising. Taking the resources from this country to benefit the privileged class in Britain is far too ingrained in their culture for them to let go."

"I understand your point, James, but there will be a new official army to support the political moves. That's probably more than I should be telling you. Trust me, James and Jack, when I say things are about to unravel for the Brits, I have to be a part of it. I have to."

The discussion went on for a number of hours, but it just kept going full circle to the same points. Conor was going nowhere until it was over. They spent three days with Conor, continuing every day to try to convince him to come back to America. They finally gave up and said their goodbyes as Conor was going back into the field to help push the drive for independence. He would not discuss any specifics about his role or the plans of the rebel forces. He had learned the value of secrecy, and even though he trusted James and Jack, he would not divulge any specifics.

"Conor, you're my brother, I love you, but you are one stubborn son of a bitch. Everyone in Boston is going to be disappointed when we come home without you."

"I know, Jim, please explain to all how I feel about what I have to do. I miss you all, and I will be back. I'll be back as soon as Ireland is free of British rule."

The three cousins bid each other a sad farewell. Again, Jack and James had no idea if they would ever see Conor again. They knew he could not be swayed by logic or reason. They also knew that he was in a dangerous country in a dangerous time. What they did not know was if he could get out of that dangerous country alive.

CHAPTER XXXIII

The execution of the leaders of the Easter Rebellion did not end the Irish Republican Brotherhood. It survived the ordeal as new leaders emerged just as dedicated and just as committed to the cause of independence as their predecessors. The victorious Sinn Fein party political leaders composed a new crop of dedicated leaders. In January of 1919, they assembled in Dublin to establish the new governing body for an independent Ireland, the Dail Eirean. They declared their independence stating that the Dail Eirean would take over for Dublin Castle in setting laws and policy for Ireland.

The new leaders were united in their desire for independence but not always on how to achieve their goal. Michael Collins was the new leader of the IRB and a cabinet member of the newly declared governing body. Collins favored an armed insurrection using a hit-and-run type of military strategy. Others like Eamon de Valera and Cathol Bougha, also members of the Dail Eirean, felt that the IRB was no longer necessary or useful. They, too, favored taking up arms, but with a more traditional military strategy. Still other members such as Arthur Griffith opposed violence as a means to achieve their common end. So while united in cause, there were differences in methods, which would result in power struggles.

The question of violence versus nonviolence was answered quickly when on the same day the Dail was declaring independence, the Tipperary Brigade of the Irish volunteer force led by Seamus Robinson pulled off the Sodoheadbeg ambush. The raiding party seized a large quantity of explosives while killing two RIC constables in the process. Thus, the war for independence had begun. The leaders in the Dail, in an effort to gain the support for the IVF, changed their name to the Irish Republican Army, a name consistent with the newly declared republic. Cathol Brugha, as minister of defense in the new government, would challenge the authority of Michael Collins in directing the IRA. Collins's power base came from his position of director of organization of the IRA, as well as his membership on the supreme council of the IRB. In this power struggle, Collins would prevail more often than not.

Brigha wanted to wage a conventional war with Britain, while Collins was in favor of a more tactical approach. He knew that the IRA forces were undermanned and underequipped to go toe to toe with the UK. His first tactic was to continue the assaults on the barracks of the Royal Irish Constabulary. This not only served the purpose of attacking isolated positions where the IRA could win the battle, it would also result in accumulating weapons as the victors would seize the arms of the vanquished. This was right up Conor's alley, having been in on the first such raid in Kilkenney.

Conor and Kevin Conley were reunited with Eamon McAleney in the town of Spiddal County, Galway. The two Americans, along with a dozen other IRA members, would form one of the raiding parties to attack RIC Barracks. Eamon McAleney would be the leader of this group. He had led these type raids prior to the Easter Uprising, as well as joining the fighting in Dublin on that fateful Easter Monday. He had served fourteen months in prison for those efforts.

As the group assembled in a Spiddal safe house, Conor had a bit of an old home week feeling. He approached his old commander with a warm smile and a salute. "Commander McAlaney, it is a pleasure and an honor to be in your command again."

"Conor Cashman, I have commanded few men of your equal" was the reply as the two men shook hands. Kevin got a similar greeting. Introductions were made all around before McAlaney got down to the business of explaining their mission. This group would be attacking a half-dozen RIC barracks in County Galway and County Mayo. The purpose would be to gain armaments and to destroy the barracks. "Some of you have been on similar missions. We will take each assignment individually with a different strategy that suits the target. We will do proper reconnaissance prior to the attack, as well as spend several days planning the attack. We don't act impulsively, we will act strategically."

Conor knew from past experience that McAleney was a thorough leader who planned every move methodically. He also knew from past experience that planning was no guarantee that there would not be casualties. In line with McAlaney's style of total preparations, the group spent the next week going through basic drills, getting to know each other. The leader was spending this preparation time to get them working together as a unit.

The unit's first target was the barracks in Clifden, County Galway. Advance work indicated that there would be six constables at the barracks early on the Monday morning of the attack. On a typical day after a brief period, three or four of those present would leave the barracks for duties around Clifden. The plan was to pick off as many constables outside the barracks as they could before rushing the building. Teams of two IRA soldiers were strategically placed around Clifden to intercept constables as they left the barracks. Conor and Kevin were positioned on Main Street, two blocks west of the barracks.

At eight thirty-five, two constables stepped out the front door of the barracks. They stood talking for a few minutes as one of them lit a cigarette. Then they split up with one of them walking west towards the two Americans who were hidden in a doorway and the other headed east where another two man IRA team would be waiting.

"I've got him," Conor said as he stepped out of the doorway. "Just cover my back."

Conor began walking toward the approaching constable. He was palming a metal club about six inches long in his right hand. As they got close to one another, Conor said good morning to the constable as he nodded his head, trying to make him feel comfortable. He kept an eye on the doorway of the barracks to make sure no additional constables would be coming out. As soon as they passed each other, Conor wheeled quickly, striking the constable over the head. In a continuous move, he caught him as he fell. Kevin ran up to help carry him into an alley, where they tied and gagged him; mission accomplished.

Similar actions took out two more constables by different teams over the next half hour. Getting the occupants down to three, McAleney decided it was time to move. Leading a party of six men, he burst into the front door with guns drawn and pointed at the three remaining men. They all surrendered without a shot. Two IRA soldiers brought a wagon up to the back door of the barracks, where the three bound and gagged constables were loaded into the back. They then took the wagon around to pick up the other three. All six were deposited a mile outside of town center in a thicket of trees, still bound and gagged. The wagon came back to the barracks, and the seized weapons were loaded into the back, covered over, and the wagon went off with McAleney and five other members on board. The whole operation was over by 11:00 a.m., when the barracks were set on fire. The entire unit regrouped that evening in the Spiddal safe house to celebrate their success.

Two more raids over the next two weeks—one in Galway, one in Mayo—netted more seized arms. These raids taking place all over the country in rural areas caused the RIC to abandon their more isolated barracks and consolidate into the cities. Thus, the last three planned raids for Conor's group were canceled. Violence continued all through 1919 and into 1920. Clashes between IRA units and units of the Royal Irish Constabulary were a constant. They became bloodier as 1920 wore on.

The civilian population was at first shocked by the aggressive actions of the IRA, but eventually, they came to support them out of patriotic sentiment. The IRA received total support from the Sinn Fein government in Dublin. The British, on the other hand, were not going to take things lying down. They declared martial law in some parts of the country to allow for internment and even execution of IRA men. In addition, they deployed a paramilitary force, the Black and Tans, to deal with the problem. This force acted in a particularly brutal fashion to IRA members and civilians alike. Their brutal response to the troubles only helped gain support for the IRA from the general population.

It also had the effect of making Michael Collins more determined, as well as more violent, in his own response. He stepped up efforts in what became phase 2 of the IRA campaign for independence. In late November of 1920, a special unit of the IRA created by Collins pulled off a mass assassination of fourteen suspected British intelligence officers in Dublin. In retaliation, a force of Black and Tans indiscriminately fired into a crowd at a football match in Dublin, killing fifteen civilians who had nothing to do with the IRA. This became known as Bloody Sunday and helped galvanize support for IRA efforts among the general population. It ushered in a bloody 1921.

CHAPTER XXXIV

Conor Cashman, like many in the IRA, was a wanted man. As such, he had to keep himself out of harm's way in terms of traveling at night under cover of darkness and staying in safe houses. The Americans who had joined the IRA to fight the British were a particular sore spot with British forces, so to capture one and bring him to trial would be sweet revenge.

After the first raid in Clifden, British military forces were dispatched to the area in an attempt to find the responsible parties. This was fairly common practice, but on this occasion, the daylight raid had generated a number of witnesses who could identify the participants. Small groups of British soldiers scoured the areas around Clifden, with eyewitnesses along to help identify any of the culprits that they encountered.

As Conor took a daylight walk through Spiddal two days after the raid, he saw to his horror a group of four British soldiers around a civilian male who was pointing at Conor. The group was no more than a couple of hundred yards away. Sensing what was happening, Conor immediately began running away. One of the soldiers commanded him to stop, and a shot was fired either at him or in the air. He was not sure. He kept running along the main street among passing civilians, quite sure that with all the human traffic around. he would be safe from gunfire. One look behind him told him that the four soldiers were in pursuit.

Spiddal was a coastal community with docks on Gallway Bay. He headed down to the docks to seek refuge, turning a corner on a side street out of sight of his pursuers. Running downhill to the docks, he passed a number of houses and took a couple of turns in order to not be in the sight line of the soldiers. Finally reaching the docks, he knew he had to take cover rather than continue running. It was low tide, and several dozen fishing boats were tied to the dock. Looking behind him and not seeing the pursuing soldiers, he jumped down into one of the boats, looking for a proper hiding place.

Behind him, the soldiers had lost sight of him and were not sure if he had taken refuge in one of the houses along the road to the docks. They decided to split up, with two of the soldiers checking the houses, the other two taking the witness down to the docks to search there. If they found him in one of the houses, the two left behind would bring him down to the docks for positive identification.

Conor looked frantically around the forty-foot fishing boat for a place to hide. He had not noticed the owner of the boat until he came out of the cabin and confronted him.

"What do you mean boarding my ship without permission? Who are you?"

"I'm a desperate man in need of help. I'm an IRA soldier being chased by British soldiers, and I need a place to hide." Conor had no idea of this man's loyalties, and he had no time to check. He waited for an answer, ready to climb back up to the dock or jump over the side if the answer was not good.

"Say no more," the man finally said. "I can hide you here." He pulled back a tarp, under which there were several buckets used to spread a chum line and a pile of fishing gear.

"Climb in behind those buckets, and I will cover you with the fishing gear and the tarp."

Conor did as he was instructed. The smell from the buckets and from the tarp was nauseating, but he had no choice but to lie still as he was covered up with fishing gear and the tarp. He lay quietly for what seemed like an eternity, listening to the captain move around his boat organizing things. His only weapon was a pocketknife with a four-inch blade. He held it, blade open, in his right hand in case he was discovered. He did not intend to go down without a fight.

Finally he heard the voices of one of the British soldiers speaking from the dock.

"Have you seen anyone running down through here, mister?"

"I'm busy getting ready to go out to sea. I have no time to be watching the goings on around the dock area."

"We are looking for a dangerous fugitive. We know he came down to this area, so we are searching the vessels until we find him."

"You don't need to search this one. I have been here working all morning, and I've seen no one."

"We will search it anyway," spoke one of the soldiers as he jumped down into the boat. The captain looked as if he wanted to object, but the second soldier stood on the dock pointing a rifle at him.

The soldier searched in the cabin and below deck before asking about the tarp. "What's under the tarp?"

"Just fishing gear. I'm a fisherman."

Conor heard the tarp being grabbed. He tightened his grip on the knife, thinking that he would surely be discovered. The tarp was pulled back. Conor was covered with so much fishing gear that he could not see the soldier. Hardly any daylight penetrated through. To the soldier, it just looked like a pile of gear behind a number of chum buckets. The smell of the buckets, when he pulled back the tarp, made him gag. It also discouraged him from looking any further. He dropped the tarp back down. Conor relaxed a bit, hoping it was over. The soldier looked up at his mate, declaring there was nothing there. With that, he climbed up on the dock.

"Don't I get an apology?" the captain asked.

"Apology?" the soldier answered. "You're lucky we don't impound the boat and arrest your stupid Irish ass just because we feel like it."

The two of them walked away with the witness in tow. The captain went back about his work, keeping an eye on the search crew as they worked their way down the dock, searching every boat. They were eventually joined by two other Brits in conducting their search.

When he was sure they were out of earshot, the captain leaned down over the tarp, telling Conor to stay put until he told him better. The four Brits stayed around the dock area for another hour and a half. Conor lay under the tarp the entire time. Finally, the captain pulled the tarp back and unpiled the fishing gear to let him out. The fresh air was marvelous as Conor came up from the sickening smell he had been covered with for hours.

"You need to stay put for a while. They have left the dock area and gone into the town, but they are still looking. You should stay here until it's dark."

"I owe you a great deal, and I don't even know your name."

"The name is Seamus Carey, and I'm always ready to help one of you IRA boys. Tell me your own name."

"I'm Conor Cashman, and you risked your life to help me. If I had been found on your boat, they would have taken you along with me."

"So, you're a Yank. What got you tangled up in our mess?"

"I'm a Yank, but as my mother used to say, I'm as Irish as Paddy's pig. Both my parents were born here in Ireland, and I think it's about time the Brits went home."

"Well, I couldn't agree more on that score. Look, stay here until dark with me, and I will go up ahead of you to see if they are still skulking around. The thing is, I think they will smell you before they see you."

"I know, I'm a bit ripe coming out from that hiding place."

"No matter, I happen to have a jug here in the cabin that will last us until dark. A few pulls off of it, and you won't be able to smell anything."

"Shouldn't I stay close to the tarp in case they come back?"

"No, the tide is coming in, so we see can over the dock. We can just keep an eye out. If they start back down here, we will have time to tuck you away again. Come on, we can drink for a spell."

With that, the two of them went into the cabin and opened up a jug. They drank until after dark, swapping stories about life as a fisherman in Ireland and life in America. After dark, Seamus Carey led the way up out of the docks into the town. He stayed thirty or forty feet ahead of Conor, looking around to see if the soldiers were still around. Not seeing them, he waved Conor ahead. When he got close enough to the safe house, he thanked Seamus for the help and headed home.

Upon his arrival, he told his mates his harrowing story of escape. The other occupants of the house told him he had to burn his clothing and take a bath before they would let him stay.

CHAPTER XXXV

Back in Salem, Jack was steadily moving to a whole new phase of life. In the spring of 1920, he began construction of two double-decker houses on the Loring Avenue property he had purchased. His plan was to have each of his two sons have a home there for their families. He and Bridget would retire and live upstairs over one of the boys. After forty years of running his business and serving as a municipal official, Jack was looking forward to a quiet retirement with Bridget and his grandchildren.

They now had three grandchildren. His son John and his wife, Clara, had a son, Joseph, and a daughter, Anna, named after her grandmother. His son Bill had a son, John, and his wife, Jane, was pregnant with their second child. Both boys were well ensconced into the post office with good-paying, secure jobs.

Brother Tom's children were all now married and moved out. His son, John, had moved into Boston, where he worked in an accounting firm. Tom's plan for retirement was to move to Boston to live near his son.

As construction moved along on Loring Avenue, Jack and Tom put the store up for sale. It being a very popular and profitable business, it did not take long for it to sell. They put it on the market in August, got an offer in September, and closed the sale in early November. At the same time, they sold the house on Becket Street to another party, closing that deal in October. So by the end of 1920, the sixty-year-old Jack and the sixty-three-year-old Tom were both retired. Tom lived in Boston, while Jack retired to Loring Avenue, living upstairs over his son Bill.

It all happened fast, but not without a good deal of emotion. The two weeks before the deal closed, while Jack and Tom were working with the new owners, Jack had a bad feeling about letting go what had been his life now for almost forty years. He would stand in the store, staring at places, picturing his mother, Johanna, working there, talking to a local customer. Or he would sit at a table where he and Anna used to sit to have tea together. He remembered the times Sullivan came up with his Uncle Pat and Pat McGowan and what a stir it would create to have the champ in town. All memories of very happy times gone by. All memories of important people in his life that were gone now.

At night, he would have the same experience remembering his young sons playing on the floor or coming home for dinner in the summertime after playing baseball all day. His son John played the piano while he and Anna sang. It was all proving to be tremendously emotional. Many nights, Bridget would sense his melancholy and sit with him, holding his hand. On one such occasion, she tried to comfort him by reminding him they were still young with a lot of good memories still to be had.

"We will have a good life after we move, Jack. The boys and the grandchildren will be right there with us. We can enjoy them more as they grow, when we are not saddled with the store."

"I know, Brid, life goes on. I just wonder where the years have gone. The great feelings Tom and I had when we first started. The support we had from Uncle Pat. The good friends who were around then who are all gone now. It's been over thirty years since Peter Grady died, and I still miss him. I miss Johanna, Uncle Pat, Sullivan, all of them."

"And you miss Anna. You can say that, Jack, I understand."

Jack put his arm around Bridget as he looked into her eyes. "I do miss Anna, Brid. Just like you do. But I have not forgotten how you saved me and the boys. We have been happy together for almost twenty years now. I love you as much as I loved Anna. You Hennesseys have a way of placing a tattoo on me that can't be removed."

With that, they sat together talking about their memories all through the night. They both knew their lives would be changing very shortly. While the new life may be grand, the memories they had would never be replaced, nor would they fade away.

CHAPTER XXXVI

By the second half of 1920 and into 1921, the violence on both sides had increased dramatically. The Black and Tans units dispatched by the British stepped up the attacks on the IRA members as well as suspected IRA members. On the other side, the IRA, under the direction of Michael Collins and Richard Mulcahy, had gone to guerilla fighting with "flying columns," attacking RIC columns and positions as well as attacks on British troops. They boldly attacked fortified police barracks as well as Black and Tans units and regular British army troops melding back into the general population after the attack. By late 1920, attacks on RIC positions had become so common and so violent that many RIC men were resigning their commissions.

To add to Britain's problems, Sinn Fein won a number of local government elections in 1920. After winning these local seats, they took over functions of government, including law enforcement, replacing RIC with Irish Republican Police. What's more, the railway workers began a boycott, refusing to transport British troops. All this was adding to the pressure on Britain to solve the crises through negotiation. To further complicate matters, the situation in the north was even more of a mess. Ulster unionists were in the majority and had no sympathy for the idea of an independent Ireland. Conflict along religious lines were worsening by the day. Loyalists attacking Catholic positions killed upward of one hundred people, burned out Catholic homes. Seven thousand Catholics were expelled from their jobs in Belfast shipyards. Things were coming to a head. Emotions on all sides in Ireland were understandably high. In England, emotions were also high, bringing pressure on Westminster to solve its issue.

Conor Cashman had taken part in a number of raids and attacks on Black and Tans units and RIC barracks over an eighteen-month period. He and Kevin Conley were both loyal IRA soldiers and were wanted by the Black and Tans units. Between attacks, they were moving from safe house to safe house. After the Galway and Mayo raids, their activities were confined to the Munster Province, where much of the action was taking place. Munster Province was one of the areas of Ireland where martial law had been declared. The two Americans took part in the ambushing of a Black and Tans auxiliary unit in Kilmichael Western Cork. The IRA unit under Tom Barry killed eighteen auxiliaries in the raid. Conor himself accounted for three of those deaths. In early 1921, Barry's men teamed with an IRA unit led by Liam Lynch in attacking a column of British soldiers, killing thirteen of them. The action was constant, and Conor was part of the "flying columns," participating in a number of the hit-and-run operations.

In March of 1921, Tom Barry's men, including the two Americans, met with Richard Mulcahy, Michael Collins's right-hand man. Mulcahy was traveling the country, meeting with active units to brief them on the overall effort and effect it was having. The purpose was to build morale while also planning actions. It was a very positive tone with which he briefed the men.

"We have taken many local positions of authority through the election of Sinn Fein party members. We are using those positions to transfer power to our own people. In addition, we are winning militarily with our guerilla-style tactics. RIC men are resigning by the dozens to escape the war. The Black and Tans units are being defeated all across the country. At home, the British people have grown tired of it all. They are bringing pressure on their government to put a stop to it."

Tom Barry asked a question, "Is there any talk of a truce or negotiations for a settlement?"

"The government of Prime Minister David Lloyd George is insisting that a truce must include the IRA surrendering our arms. Mr. DeValera told him where he could stick that idea."

The group enjoyed that remark. After a bit more discussion, Mulcahy went into the discussion of a major assignment for Barry's unit.

"There is a major British army force here in Munster that has been operating pretty much unobstructed. They have been backing up the play of Black and Tans units throughout the province, giving them support and strength. We have information that they will be on the move in a few days. We want to hit them hard with a coordinated ambush. We want this unit, as well as Liam Lynch's unit, to hit them with a one-two punch at Crossbarry."

Mulcahy went into more detail, but saved much of the strategy for a meeting planned for the next morning with Tom Barry and Liam Lynch. Conor Cashman could not have been more excited about the upcoming ambush. This was to be an attack on a column of the British regular army, the most highly trained fighters involved in the war. Conor saw it as a great challenge.

"You know, Kevin, if Mulcahy came down here to meet with us, this has to be a big deal."

"I really like the idea of teaming up with those boys in Lynch's unit. Good fighters, every one."

"We'll see what comes out of tomorrow's meeting, but I for one can't wait for the action."

Kevin said jokingly, "You're getting to be a bit bloodthirsty, Conor. It's a bit scary."

Conor just smiled at his friend.

The next afternoon, Tom Barry talked to his men about the plan of attack. The ambush would take place in three days at Crossbarry. They would hit the British column early in the morning as they marched through Crossbarry. Barry's unit was less than a half day's march from the attack site. Lynch's unit was a good day away. They planned to meet up the night before. Barry had one hundred or so men, while Lynch had a bit larger force of about one hundred fifty men. Still, even combined, they would be outnumbered four or five to one. This being the case, it would be a planned surprise hit-and-run. They would open fire on the British soldiers from both sides of the road, take out as many as possible with the first volley, then exchange fire for four or five rounds before fleeing in several different directions, making it difficult for the Brits to give chase. They would regroup in a designated area seventeen miles from the attack site the next day.

It all sounded pretty well planned out, but as the saying goes, the best-laid plan will often go asunder. Barry's men waited in vain the night before the planned attack for Lynch's men to show. What they did not know was that Lynch had run into a Black and Tans unit, who engaged them in an extended bloody gun battle. By four in the morning, it was clear they would not be joining in the ambush. Barry decided that he wanted to carry out the plan without Lynch. So he dispatched half of his troops on each side of the road with the same instructions for the ambush. Barry's unit had pulled off a number of successful hit-and-run attacks of this type, so he felt confident. Sometimes too much success can breed overconfidence.

Kevin Conley was very apprehensive about going it alone. "Conor, we were already outnumbered even with Lynch. Now we are outnumbered ten or twelve to one."

"It's a hit-and-run, Kevin. We take out seventy or eighty men with the first attack. Maybe pick off twenty or more in the ensuing exchange, then we bolt. You know from past experience they won't follow us for more than a half mile."

"I still don't like it, Conor. Lynch not showing up is a bad omen."

Conor smiled at this. "You wouldn't be Irish if you weren't superstitious."

With that, they lay in waiting for the British forces. They did not have to wait long. A column of twelve hundred men came noisily toward their position before nine o'clock. The troops on both sides of the road held their fire until they had the bulk of the column in a cross fire position. On the signal, Barry's men opened fire from behind hedges, trees, and rocks where they were hiding. As planned, the opening round took out a good number of unsuspecting soldiers. Before the men could fire a second round, the British troops dropped to one knee and returned fire. A general gun battle followed, with casualties on both sides. Conor only got off two rounds before being hit high up on the right side of his chest. The bullet knocked him down, rendering him unconscious. Kevin went to his side, kneeling down to see if he was still alive. Feeling a pulse in his neck, Kevin decided he needed to get him out of there.

Meanwhile the rear of the British column had broken off on both sides of the road, aiming to encircle the rebels. Seeing this maneuver taking shape, the rebel leaders called for a withdrawal even as they directed their fire against the encircling British troops. The main part of the column, seeing the retreat taking shape, charged the rebel positions. It was looking very much like a route.

Kevin Conley, in the midst of all this, had picked up his friend Conor, put him over his shoulder, and began moving away from the fray. He had a head start on both the retreating rebels and the charging British. A quarter of a mile from his position stood a farmhouse with a large barn. His goal was to make it to the barn. The fighting was going on behind him as the rest of the force fought the attackers as they made their retreat. Kevin stayed ahead of them, making it to the barn with Conor on his shoulder. He climbed into the loft, laid Conor down, and worked to stop the bleeding on Conor's wound. He tore off his shirt, ripping it apart to use it as bandages. Conor was bleeding badly. Kevin knew he had to stop the blood flow.

The side of the road that Conor and Kevin helped man was the same side Tom Barry was holding down. He and his men were able to stave off the attempt at encircling and make an escape as they fired on their pursuers. The forty men on the other side of the road were not so lucky. Twelve were battlefield casualties, the rest captured and eventually executed for treason. Munster, being under martial law at time, the trials and executions took less than two weeks.

Barry lost fourteen of his fifty-two men while the rest escaped, carrying four wounded, not counting Conor. The entire operation resulted in Barry's unit losing over half his men while inflicting just under sixty casualties on the British forces. Hardly the success they had planned. Barry would later confess that when the Lynch forces did not arrive, he should have canceled the mission.

The British troops entered the barn where Kevin was hiding as they searched for fleeing rebels. Kevin covered himself and Conor in hay in the back of the loft. He lay still under the hay listening as a British soldier climbed the ladder to look into the loft. Kevin held his breath and hoped that Conor would not make any noise. Somehow they managed to avoid capture. When the troops left, he had his second problem of keeping Conor alive. He used his own torn shirt to try to stop the bleeding. Hours later, when things settled down and the troops had gone, he approached the farmhouse for help. His knock on the door was answered by the owner of the farm, a Mr. Lynch who, thankfully, was a supporter of the cause. He said his family had been enclosed in the farmhouse to escape the gunfire.

"I have a man in the barn who is badly wounded and in need of a doctor."

Kevin had no idea how he would be received by the family. Many Irish were not in support of its rebel cause.

Lynch replied, "I will send my son for a doctor. You and I should bring your friend in the house where we can treat the wounds."

Kevin and his host carried Conor into the house, where Mrs. Lynch looked at the wound. She had spent some time working with the local doctor and knew enough medicine to know that the wound did not look good.

"This is a bad wound your friend has. I do not know that he will survive it."

"Please do what you can before the doctor gets here. It's very important to me that Conor lives."

An exhausted Kevin Conley looked at Mrs. Lynch with a pleading look that touched her heart.

She washed the wound with hot water, bandaged him as best she could, and they all sat waiting for the doctor. Kevin sat in a chair next to his friend's bed. Conor remained unconscious. He did not look good, and nobody in the room was optimistic about his survival.

CHAPTER XXXVII

Communication systems were not as fast as they are today, but it still did not take long for word to get back to America that Conor had once again been shot. Kevin Conley had gotten word to Conor's cousin, Sean, and that word had been passed on by cablegram to James Cashman in Boston. He immediately called Jack with the news.

"How bad is it this time, James?"

"It's very bad. He cannot be transferred to Sean Cashman's because he is far too weak."

"Okay, we have to go back over to get him. This time we cannot take no for an answer."

"At this point, Jack, I don't know if we would be going to bring Conor back, or Conor's body back."

"It's that bad?"

"It is that bad. I think we have to wait to see if his condition improves before we make any plans. If he survives, we will need to wait until he's in a condition that we can bring him home. If he does not survive, we will be going to bring his body home."

"We will pray for him, Jim. Hopefully, the good Lord will save him."

Jack passed the news on to his sons, to Tom's family, and to Bridget. The entire McCarthy clan would indeed be praying for Conor's recovery. Jack awaited word from his cousin concerning the upcoming trip to Ireland that would have to be made whatever way things went with Conor.

In Ireland, it was weeks of touch-and-go, with Conor having to stay in the Lynch's farmhouse. It was a very lucky draw for Kevin to have ended up with this family. The Lynch family were loyal Republicans who gave full support to the cause of Irish independence. In his younger years, Liam Lynch, the family patriarch, had been a member of the Irish Volunteer Brotherhood. So they gave full support to hiding both Conor and Kevin, as well as helping to try to keep Conor alive. The local doctor had removed the bullet and dressed the wound. He came by as often as his schedule allowed, but for weeks, Conor lay in bed close to death with the doctor giving no assurances that he would recover.

Meanwhile, the fighting continued as pressure continued to build on the Lloyd George government in London to do something to bring it to an end. King George V, in a speech in Belfast, called for a reconciliation on all sides. It was an unexpected olive branch offering from the British monarch. The speech was one of several signs that British resolve was weakening. The continuing guerilla warfare with no end in sight was having its effects on the British people.

Finally, after eighteen days of nobody being able to predict he would recover, Conor took a positive turn. His on-again-off-again fever went away for good as he began to slowly regain his strength. Kevin had stayed with him the entire time. After receiving the first positive report from the doctor, he went into his friend's room to talk about the next steps. He felt like a great weight had been lifted from him as for the first time in weeks he felt confident his friend was going to make it.

"Well, it looks as if your stubborn, ornery ass is going to survive yet again."

"Don't sound so bloody happy about it, you prick."

"Well, you lying around here doing nothing is cramping my own style. I need some action."

"Me, too. When can I get back at it? What does the doctor say?"

"I think your fighting days are over, me man. It will be at least two or three weeks before we can move you to your cousin Sean's place. Even then, you will not be fit for duty for a good long while."

"Bullshit, Kevin, I've got plenty of fight left in me. I will be soon back at it."

Conor tried to sit up as he said this, wincing in pain, and he sat back down.

Kevin answered him in a very serious tone, "Conor, you came very close to dying. You are not completely out of the woods even now. It will be a long recovery for you this time, much longer than the last."

Conor understood the seriousness with which this message was delivered by his friend to mean that he had better believe every word. It was not what he wanted to hear, but he knew he should take it as the gospel truth.

"That is a very sad message you deliver, Kevin." Conor closed his eyes, trying to block out the reality of the situation.

Three weeks later, in mid-June, Conor was moved into his cousin Sean's farmhouse. The IRA provided a wagon, as well as half-dozen armed men to facilitate the move. Kevin had worked every day on the Lynch farm to help thank them for taking care of Conor. Both Americans expressed their gratitude for all the support they received from the Lynch family.

At Sean Cashman's farm, the routine was the same. Kevin helped out with the work at the farm while Conor continued to recover. He was becoming a well-trained, valuable farmhand, not that it was the profession he would voluntarily choose. The work was hard and never seemed to be finished.

As soon as they had arrived at the Cashman farm, word was sent to Boston about his arrival. His brothers, James and John, began discussions with Jack about going over to Ireland on a rescue mission. "This time, we do not take no for answer," James began.

"Absolutely right, James. This time, he comes home. I think we should wait a few weeks to make sure he is all right to travel." Jack said.

"Remember, Jack, that he is still very probably a wanted man in Ireland. Getting him out may not be all that easy."

"I had not thought of that, but you, of course, are right. We will have to give that some consideration as well." The last thing they wanted was to have Conor arrested and tried for treason.

James added, "I'm sure we can get some helpful suggestions on getting him out from his friends in the IRA."

With that, they decided to keep close tabs on the process of his recovery. As soon as the word came that he was able to be moved, they would go over. The issue of how to get him out of the country would be dealt with when they got there. Thankfully, with all the fighting going on, British officials had no chance to concentrate on tracking down wanted men with Conor. Staying with his relatives, he would not have been that difficult to find.

CHAPTER XXXVIII

By the latter part of June, Conor was taking long walks as his recovery was progressing faster than expected. Kevin was learning a lot more about farming than he ever wanted to know. By this time, Conor was feeling like he was ready to get back into action. That idea ran into a road block when Jack McCarthy and Conor's brother James showed up on July 5. Their arrival was a planned surprise to Conor. Sean had kept the two apprised of Conor's progress, so Sean knew they were coming. At James's request, he had kept the news from Conor.

They arrived at the farmhouse as Kevin and Conor were returning from a walk. Both were surprised to see them.

"What the hell are you two doing here, and why wasn't I told you were coming?"

"Well, Conor, Jack and I thought it better to surprise you."

"You surprised me because you figured if I had any advance notice, I would not be here when you arrived."

"Well, there's that too," Jack answered.

Conor knew exactly why they were in Ireland, and he knew what was coming from them.

"Conor, it's time you came home." James got right to the point. "You've taken two bullets over here, you nearly died this time. It's time to come home where you belong."

Conor looked at his older brother without speaking for a long moment. He knew it made sense for him to return to Boston. On the other hand, he did not want to leave until the battle was won. He was still not at full strength. They could tell that by looking at him. He had lost a lot of weight and strength during the recovery period.

It would be a difficult argument for him to win. So he decided to go for a delay.

"Look, James, Kevin and I have been helping Sean on the farm. He and his two sons, Martin and Tim, would love to spend some time with you and Jack. Plus there are a whole pack of Cashman relatives around here, so why don't you let me think about this while we all enjoy spending some time with our Irish relatives." Conor had a pleading expression as he spoke. It was obvious he did not want to leave, but he didn't want to get into the discussion at that moment.

Right on cue, Sean and his oldest son, Martin, came out of the barn to greet their American cousins.

"Jack, James, you made it. It's so great to see the two of you. Everyone is going to be glad to see the two of you," he spoke as he shook hands with his two cousins.

"It's great to see you, Sean and Martin. We thank you for taking care of our prodigal son, or should I say, prodigal brother," James responded.

"We will give you a day to rest up, then have the clan over for a 'welcome home' party for you two Yanks." Sean was smiling broadly, happy with the proposal of getting everyone together. The enthusiasm of Sean was welcomed by Conor, who smiled broadly. His hosts were playing right into his hands.

The two Americans agreed that would be a great opportunity to see all their relatives. For his part, Conor liked the idea because it would give him more time to regain his strength so he could offer a stronger case for staying in Ireland.

It took a couple of days to get the bulk of the Cashman clan to Sean's farm for a welcoming party for Jack and James. Food and drink were plentiful as the two Americans renewed acquaintances with cousins and met some new cousins who had arrived since their last visit. Many of those who came were very familiar with Conor's involvement in the war, but they had no idea he had been wounded or that he was staying at Sean's while he recovered. It had been kept quiet for obvious reasons. Even fellow Cashmans were not told about Conor's stay at Sean's.

As always, there were many questions about life in America. Everyone wanted to know how Jay and Eamon, the two brothers who had gone to America to work for Cashman Brothers, were doing. Both, of course, were now married with children of their own. Pictures from America were passed around, and pictures from Ireland were handed out to be brought back home.

The most interesting and timely topic of conversation was the word that the country was abuzz with the rumor that discussions had begun on a proposal for a cease-fire. It was a rumor confirmed by a number of attendees, so it seemed to have some validity. Jack and James gave each other a knowing look as they heard this news. A truce would give them additional reasoning for Conor to come back to America. As the night wore on, there was plenty of song and camaraderie. It was late in the evening when things finally broke up. Jack and James decided to hold off any discussion with Conor until morning.

At breakfast, James began the conversation. "Conor, there is apparently a movement afoot to call a truce. It's all the more reason for you to come back with us."

"That's a rumor, brother, not a fact. Besides, a truce would be temporary."

Then they got support from a surprising source as Kevin Conley spoke. "I'm ready to go home, Conor. We have been here a long time. If there is a truce, and it's a temporary solution, we can come back. But I'm ready for a break."

Jack, James and especially Conor were all caught by surprise by Kevin's comments. They all exchanged looks until finally Jack added, "Your brother in arms makes a lot of sense, Conor."

Conor nodded at his brother. "Okay, James, but I reserve to myself the right to come back if there either is no truce, or if there is one but fighting resumes."

"You're a grown man, my brother. I cannot tell you what you can and can't do, but no one can ever question that you did your part. No one can ever question your courage or commitment. We are all proud of you, but we all want you home."

With that, the plans were made to bring Kevin and Conor home. They sat with Sean and Martin for several hours plotting out a course of action to get the two fugitives out of the country. They both had to travel under false names as they were both still wanted men. There were some tense moments at the boarding of the ship at Cobh Harbor. British authorities at the docks had to be carefully avoided. The two wanted men lost themselves as best they could within the crowd of people. Keeping their heads down, doing the best they could to be invisible. They were all successful in boarding the ship to America. Conor was headed home for the first time in more than seven years. He was not leaving entirely by choice, but still he was anxious to see Boston again.

Conor Cashman and Kevin Conley were not the only Irish Americans to participate in the fighting for independence. Help from the US to Ireland began during the famine when Britain turned its back on the suffering and starving. America was the first nation to step up to send help. Over the years following the famine, Irish American groups sent money as well as armaments to the Republican forces working toward an independent Ireland. During the fighting, a good few Irish Americans, like Conor and Kevin, took up arms. While they had made a new life in a new country, many carried the scars of the famine, never forgetting from whence they came.

CHAPTER XXXIX

As Conor headed home, discussions had indeed begun on a cease-fire. On July 11, 1921, a delegation led by Eamon DeValera, on behalf of the Irish forces, met with General MacReady, the British Commander in Chief for Ireland, and agreed to a truce. While IRA forces saw it as only a temporary cease-fire, it did give them an opportunity to increase recruitment efforts, as well as to train volunteers in the open. The result was that the IRA increased its numbers quickly to seventy-two-thousand-plus volunteers. It was clear that the IRA forces saw the truce as temporary. They would be well prepared when fighting resumed.

This ongoing activity and rising support among the Irish people increased the pressure on London to settle the issue. It was obvious to all that the truce was not going to have the effect of reducing the enthusiasm of the IRA, so negotiations on an Anglo-Irish treaty began in the late fall of 1921. The Irish delegation was headed by Arthur Griffith and Michael Collins.

A fully recovered Conor Cashman followed the news of these events daily. He was prepared to go back to Ireland the moment talks broke down and fighting resumed. He spoke daily with his cousin, Jack, as they summarized their thoughts on where the talks would end up. Jack sometimes felt that his cousin was rooting for the talks to fail so that he could get back into action. Conor insisted that this was not the case. Yet it was obvious that if it did resume, Conor would be catching the first boat to Ireland.

The word came through in December that an Anglo-Irish treaty had been signed. The treaty created the Irish Free State that replaced the self-declared Irish Republic of 1919. The free state included twenty-six counties out of Ireland's thirty-two. Under the treaty, Northern

Ireland was given the option of remaining in the UK. The Northern Ireland parliament chose this option. A boundary commission was set up to establish the boundary between Northern Ireland and the Southern Ireland Free State.

Conor was not pleased with the agreement. He and Jack discussed the terms soon after they learned of the specifics. "Collins and Griffith sold out," Conor lamented. "This idea of a separate Ulster Province will never work. It will be a problem for years to come, so they should deal with it now."

"We have achieved the objective of an Irish state free of British rule, no more edicts from Dublin Castle, British troops will be pulled out. These have been the good results, Conor. This is the goal we have worked for all these years."

"I guarantee you, Jack, that this treaty will be a very tough sell to many who have fought the battle."

While a majority voted to accept the treaty, Conor proved to be right in his assessment. Many in the IRA were not happy with the settlement. Collins tried to ease the dissension by supporting a clandestine campaign against Northern Ireland. These would be the last major spasms of violence. IRA offensives here failed to unite the six counties into the Irish Free State. The civil unrest with the Republican forces gave Conor a desire to go back to join the unrest. He agreed with the antitreaty side, but was not clear what positive effect a civil war would bring. The debates with his brothers and, more often, his cousin Jack continued.

"I tell you, Conor, no good can come from continued fighting. Especially if we are fighting amongst ourselves."

"It just does not seem to me that we have accomplished our objectives. It's like we are halfway there."

"You're wrong, Conor. When things all settle out, we will have arrived at the point we have all been seeking for all these years, a free, independent Ireland."

Conor remained skeptical, but he remained in Boston, working every day for Cashman Brothers. He and Jack continued to watch closely as events unfolded. They continued to debate the matter with each making their case. As 1922 moved on, it became clearer that

Jack's side was proving to be right. The final six thousand British troops were removed from Ireland. The Irish Free State government was established and began functioning. The violence did not end completely but did lessen considerably in the south. Conor proved to be right in his criticism of the six-county divide in Ulster. Northern Ireland continued to be an issue with IRA forces intent on a united Ireland, refusing to accept the split. At the same time, majority protestants continued the oppression of minority Catholics in Northern Ireland. Apart from the Northern Ireland issue, the treaty was proving to be working out as the established Irish Free State was the first fully independent functional Irish state in recorded history.

As life went on in Massachusetts for the McCarthys and the Cashmans, they continued to discuss the Irish issues as if they were sitting in Cork. Local and national issues were not ignored, but when the clans got together, the talk would always end up with comments about a free Ireland.

Jack had retired with Bridget to their new home on Loring Avenue. They spent much of their time with the grandchildren. John and Clara had three boys and one girl; Bill and his wife had two boys and a girl. The seven grandchildren filled their days. They had settled into a quiet, peaceful retirement.

Tom had retired with Mary to Boston, living next door to his son John. Margaret and Molly were not as close by, one in Fall River, the other in Brockton, but John's three youngsters kept Tom and Mary busy.

Conor melded right into the Cashman Brothers Construction Company, working with his brothers to help build a very large successful business. He never married, but there were plenty of Cashman relatives nearby with whom to share good times. All the Cashmans and McCarthys were very proud of their contribution to the cause of Ireland's freedom. They had all been active members of the Fenian Brotherhood. They had all contributed a fair amount of money over the years to their brothers and sisters fighting for the cause. As good as they felt about their own contributions, they were all particularly proud of the twice-wounded Conor Cashman. His heroics in the battle for freedom of their native land would long be told around dinner tables of the Cashmans and McCarthys.

CHAPTER XXXX

In 1849, during a flood of Irish immigration brought about by the great famine, three immigrants came over to America on the *Nautilus*. One man from Skibereen named McCarthy, and a brother and sister from Cork named Cashman. Mr. McCarthy was illiterate and unskilled. The Cashmans were able to read and write, and Mr. Cashman had worked and was skilled in the building trades.

They left a country that was in an absolutely tragic situation. People were literally starving in the streets. Complete families wiped out by the great hunger. They arrived in a country that did not want them. A country where they were looked down upon, ridiculed, and insulted. A country where they were attacked and denigrated in the press, where they couldn't find work.

Mr. McCarthy died young in an accident, leaving his wife, Johanna Cashman, a young widow with two young boys. She and her sons lived in poverty, renting a small shanty next to a leather factory.

In spite of all of these hardships, all of these adversities, they persevered. They shook off the insults, the ridicule. They worked hard. They did whatever needed to be done to succeed. They were purely and simply hardworking, honest people who refused to quit, refused to give in, and refused to let the adversity beat them. In the end, they succeeded. One family opened and operated a business in Salem that enjoyed a forty-year successful run. One family member became a very influential civic leader, the other family built the largest, most successful construction company in Massachusetts. Immigrants who arrived with nothing, but grew their businesses, raised their families, and contributed greatly to the building of the nation.

This type history is not unique to these three immigrants or to the Irish people. Many ethnic groups have come to America, overcome adversity, been successful, and contributed greatly to the building of a great nation. Still, as new waves of immigrants have arrived, history seems to repeat itself with the same insults, the same group characterization, the same attempts to degrade them as a group. It seems like America never learns from that same mistake.

While the story of Irish immigrants in America is similar to many other groups, they were set apart in the concern for the troubles in their native country. The scars from the famine that came with them to America kept them dedicated to seeing Ireland achieve its independence. Irish-American groups contributed greatly to the success of that drive for independence. Their success in America helped make it all possible. In a very real sense, the United States is a country built by immigrants. Those very same Irish immigrants who helped build the United States also helped build Ireland.

ABOUT THE AUTHOR

 Jack Cashman is retired from a long career in business and public service in Maine. He is a longtime student of Irish history, and both his father's ancestors and his mother's ancestors immigrated from Ireland to escape the famine and settled in Salem, Massachusetts. So Jack wrote his first novel about the struggles of an Irish immigrant family and Ireland's drive for independence.

Jack lives in Hampden, Maine, with his wife, Betty, close to his two sons and five granddaughters.

CPSIA information can be obtained
at www.ICGtesting.com
Printed in the USA
FSHW021454091218
54302FS